"I bet your hair and nails are always perfect," Jared teased

"Is there something wrong with a professional appearance?"

"Not when you're being professional, I guess. But I think—and maybe this is just me—you'd look great messed up."

"Messed up?"

"Maybe mussed up." Jared leaned close. "You know, tousled, disheveled..." He stroked Victoria's cheek with the tip of his finger. "Thoroughly pleasured."

Heat raced through her body. "Are you always this forward with women you've just met?"

He grinned. "Not always."

"Most of the time, I bet you are."

She wished she could find a reason to step away from him and not give in to the urge to touch him. Still, she laid her palm on his chest. "You aren't my type."

"You aren't mine, either."

But he wrapped his arm around her and kissed her anyway.

Dear Reader,

Welcome to the beach and more tales from the Robin Hood gang! My trio of friends, like the legendary characters, are ready to fight injustice again.

But while the concept seems simple, the solution isn't.

In this chapter, the ladies are escaping the stifling NYC heat and are off to the shore for balmy breezes, although Victoria isn't the toes-in-the-sand, beer-in-my-hand type. She's in beautiful, peaceful Southampton to do what else—work!

Unfortunately, her host—and a wily jewel thief— have other plans.

Victoria has the support of her best buds, of course, and the added perk of a gorgeous, adventurous cowboy Jared McKenna, who can't keep his hands off her, but in between moonlit cruises, she discovers everything is changing. Her perception of right and wrong, her realization of what really matters in life, and the love she might find in a very unlikely place.

Don't miss the exciting conclusion of the Flirting with Justice series; Calla and Devin's story, *Undone by Moonlight,* is arriving in September.

Wendy Etherington

Wendy Etherington

BREATHLESS ON THE BEACH

Recycling programs
for this product may
not exist in your area.

ISBN-13: 978-0-373-79701-1

BREATHLESS ON THE BEACH

ABOUT THE AUTHOR

Wendy Etherington was born and raised in the deep South—and she has the fried-chicken recipes and NAS-CAR ticket stubs to prove it. An author of nearly thirty books, she writes full-time from her home in South Carolina, where she lives with her husband, two daughters and an energetic shih tzu named Cody. She can be reached via her website, www.wendyetherington.com. Or follow her on Twitter @wendyeth.

Books by Wendy Etherington

HARLEQUIN BLAZE

HARLEQUIN NASCAR

*Flirting with Justice

To get the inside scoop on Harlequin Blaze and its talented writers, be sure to check out blazeauthors.com.

All backlist available in ebook. Don't miss any of our special offers. Write to us at the following address for information on our newest releases.

Harlequin Reader Service
U.S.: 3010 Walden Ave., P.O. Box 1325, Buffalo, NY 14269
Canadian: P.O. Box 609, Fort Erie, Ont. L2A 5X3

1

"It is the spirit and not the form of law that keeps justice alive."

—Earl Warren

New York Tattletale
Labor Day Weekend Edition
Those Who Have, Do!
by Peeps Galloway, Gossipmonger (And proud of it!)
Well, kids, with summer winding down, tradition dictates the posh and influential of NYC gather in Southampton for one last gasp of fun and sun.

I hear (from sources I'd have to give away my priceless collection of original Versace gowns if I revealed—not gonna happen, BTW!) there's a new product coming from the prestigious firm of Rutherford Security that'll change the way the rich and famous store their gems and secrets.

No doubt more will be heard by those lucky enough to have received a coveted invite to the longtime Southampton socialite Rose Rutherford's fabulous house party.

Mrs. Rutherford's husband, Raymond, made his

money in Texas oil in the eighties, but though he met his fate nearly fifteen years ago in the arms of his stripper mistress, he had the decency to invest in lucrative beach-front property, providing Rose with the perfect locale for entertaining. Among the high-end guests will be her son, Richard (yes, everyone in the family has the *R* moniker), who chose the lovely and tasteful Ruthanne as a mate.

Also of interest on the guest list is the inclusion of two (yes, *dos!*) executives from Coleman Public Relations. Both Peter Standish and Victoria Holmes (of the Holmes Family Cardiac Wing at Midtown Memorial) are attending the weekend house party.

Is Mrs. Rutherford just that generous to PR execs or do we smell heated competition for something?

Hmm...

Certainly jealousy will rear its ugly (but column-worthy) head, which is much more fun than a leisurely cocktail hour by the pool, anyway. So stay tuned!

On the agenda are wild water excursions provided by Flaming Arrow Adventure Tours. Calls from this office by yours truly for details were unreturned (as if *that* would deter your loyal and tireless columnist!?!), but don't you worry, dear readers, I'm on the case!

I'm informed that Jet Ski riding, scuba diving, boating and other activities involving the potential for bodily harm have been scheduled. (Dear heaven, count me out!) But then I hear the adventure guide is none other than Jared McKenna, and trust me, rabid followers, he is hot, hot, smokin' hot. So maybe extreme sports are a hobby to consider after all...

Kiss and tell—*please!*

—Peeps

P.S. Catering to be provided by Shelby Dixon (recently highlighted in this column!)

TAKING HER FOCUS OFF THE clogged Manhattan traffic at a stoplight, Victoria Holmes shifted her hard, determined gaze between her two best friends. "I'm getting this contract or else."

"Or else what?" Calla Tucker asked, folding up her newspaper and placing it neatly on her lap.

"Or else she blames us," Shelby Dixon answered.

Pleased her pals had gotten the point so quickly, Victoria stared through the windshield of her Mercedes and ordered her stomach to cease its churning.

She was going to get the contract—*and* the promotion. Like her mother before her, she'd given everything to Coleman PR.

But your mother's a legend, and you don't quite measure up, do you?

Didn't she? Victoria always worked nights, weekends, holidays. She brought in high-dollar clients with high-dollar campaigns. She oozed ambition and confidence, even though her mother had been the youngest senior VP in the history of the firm and nobody ever let Victoria forget it.

She schmoozed. She demurred when necessary. She represented the firm with the utmost in professionalism. She deserved her own senior VP title and corner office. She'd earned the right to step from behind her mother's long shadow and prove she hadn't clung to her coattails to attain success.

Didn't she?

"This Rutherford contract will put me over the edge," she muttered.

"She's talking to herself again," Calla said from the backseat.

"Let her be," Shelby said. "She's barely slept in the last week. She's punchy."

Victoria scowled. "You both know I can hear you, don't you?"

Calla patted Victoria's shoulder. "Don't worry, sister. We've got your back."

Shelby laughed. "And I've got your stomach."

Despite her mood, Victoria was grateful for her friends' support. As a caterer, Shelby was giving up the long weekend with her live-in boyfriend to serve as chef to the Rutherford house party they were attending in Southampton. Calla, a travel writer, was hoping to make good use of both her camera and her keyboard.

"You know I appreciate you guys coming with me," Victoria said, making an effort to soften her tone. "I need these meetings to go smoothly."

"Hey, I'm just happy to see the Rutherford estate." Calla sounded slightly awestruck. "It's been featured in *Architectural Views* countless times over the years. Maybe I'll get my own magazine piece out of this."

"And I'm grateful for the business," Shelby said. "After the June bridal season it was a long, booking-free summer."

"You were exhausted after all those weddings," Calla pointed out. "You needed a break."

"Why doesn't that rich lover of yours recommend you to all his rich friends?" Victoria asked.

"He does, but he's got a business of his own to run. Besides, just like most of the friends you recommend, the affluent have been in the Hamptons all summer. I'm too small of an operation to be hauling equipment and supplies out there every weekend."

"I'm sure Rose Rutherford's gourmet kitchen has everything we need," Calla said.

"The housekeeper assures me they do," Shelby explained. "Plus, she was willing to let my food suppliers deliver everything directly, so I didn't have to bring the van."

"I'm not arriving at the Rutherford estate in a catering van," Victoria insisted, cutting between two cabs to take the next right onto East Thirty-second.

"Heaven forbid anybody thinks you have a domestic for a friend," Calla teased.

Victoria met Calla's gaze with a glare in the rearview mirror. "I'm not a snob. Appearance is important for getting this contract."

"And I'm not a domestic," Shelby stated firmly. Then added, "Not that there's anything wrong with being one…"

Shelby turned and exchanged a meaningful look with Calla.

"I saw that," Victoria said. "Since I'm the one who's driving, aren't you two worried about me being both deaf and blind?"

Shelby cleared her throat. "I was reminding Calla that this weekend is about you getting the Rutherford Securities contract, even though she could be tanning and ogling lifeguards, and I could be naked between the sheets in a beachside hotel with my man."

"Wow, that was *some* look," Victoria said drily.

"Have you heard any more about Coleman Sr.'s rumored retirement?" Shelby asked, obviously guessing Victoria's temper was too cutting for humor.

She nodded. "They're announcing next week after the holiday. I got it straight from his secretary."

"Why'd she tell you?" Calla asked.

"Because I, unlike her boss, never forget her birthday or Secretary's Day, or that her favorite flowers are daisies or that she likes chocolates filled with caramel."

Shelby angled her head. "How do you remember all that?"

Victoria shrugged. "I have a file on everybody. Trust me, ladies, the key to a smooth ride up the corporate ladder is making nice with the real power brokers—the assistants."

Which she'd learned straight from The Legend, namely her mother. The reminder dulled her resentment. Victoria didn't expect people to pity her because she had to live up to excellence.

But besides her mom, there was her attorney father, her cardiac surgeon grandfather and the Holmes foundation run by her grandmother and cousin to measure her success against. All in all, a pretty daunting yardstick.

"So when Coleman Sr. retires," Shelby said, "Coleman Jr. inherits the long-awaited president's position, and their valuable client Rutherford Securities is up for grabs."

Victoria's mouth went dry with anticipation. "And the senior VP corner office gets a new occupant."

Shelby patted her leg. "You'll get it. Nobody works harder than you. Don't worry."

But Victoria was worried.

Thanks to her influential family connections, she had been invited by the Rutherfords to their annual Labor Day weekend party. She was going to use the opportunity to talk to Richard, Rose's son, about a strategy to promote an innovative new product that Rutherford Securities had developed.

The future of her career and her reputation among her infamously affluent family rested on the next few days.

Calla leaned forward between them. "So what cool security thing does ole Rich need a PR strategy for? I loved those commercials where the chimpanzee disables the security system by banging on the control panel."

Victoria winced. She had a strict policy against silly animals in campaigns, particularly in a serious industry like home and business security. "That was an ad for motion sensor cameras." One Coleman Sr. had come up with, yet another reason it was time for him to retire and let her take over the account.

Shelby looked up from the list she'd been scribbling. "Would the police or animal control have been alerted about an intrusion?"

"Both, maybe. But this new venture for Rutherford is completely different." Victoria pressed her lips together. The idea seemed out-of-date to her, but she'd once done a campaign for bubble gum that changed colors the longer a kid chewed it. The actual product was irrelevant. "It's a safe."

"Safe from what?" Calla asked.

Without success, Victoria fought the blush—*a blush*—creeping across her face. "Not safe from anything. A *safe*."

Her friends exchanged another one of *those* looks just before Shelby tapped her pen against her lips. "One of those big, heavy, metal things you store valuables in?"

Victoria flexed her hands on the steering wheel. "Yes."

"Well, that's..." Shelby began.

"Innovative," Calla finished.

"Oh, please stop," Victoria said. "It's on the left side of nutty. But with banks failing and consumer confidence in traditional investments falling, it might strike a chord."

"Better than burying your cash in the backyard," Calla said.

Shelby nodded. "Especially since I don't have a backyard."

"Supposedly, this one's got a state-of-the-art computer chip that makes the dial and tumbler thing passé," Victoria said, aware the simpleness of the product was going to be the biggest challenge to overcome. "Regardless, Richard's going to invest a lot of money to convince people this is a must-have electronic gadget."

"Invest with you," Calla said a little too brightly.

"Yeah." Victoria got on I-495 and headed east. An old-school product with a futuristic upgrade? This was exactly the campaign that might, just might, outpace her mother's crazy-at-the-time idea of investing in websites to promote things. "'Cause I deserve it. Don't I?"

JARED MCKENNA WIPED SWEAT OFF his brow as he tied the fourth and last Jet Ski to the Rutherford estate's dock.

Despite the privileged puffballs he'd be entertaining all weekend, the hard work was relished and the view appreciated. A few cottony clouds hovered in the broad blue sky. Whitecaps dotted the blue-green Atlantic and looked like a welcome respite from the oppressive heat enveloping the city and coast for weeks.

Originating from Montana, Jared wasn't sure he'd ever get used to the humidity of the East, but a breeze kicked up, cooling his face. The Jet Skis bobbed merrily in the sea, and he couldn't imagine being anywhere else.

Though the warmth of the sun called, he figured he'd better check in with everybody at the house.

He walked up the dock and along the sidewalk to the back door and found Marion Keegan, the housekeeper, bustling around the kitchen. "How's the prettiest lady in New York?"

Her pale face turned red. "You're a devil," she said in a musical Irish accent.

He grinned. "I try, Mrs. K, I try."

She straightened an already perfect bowl of fruit that was sitting on the center island, then pulled a pitcher of lemonade from the fridge and poured him a glass. "We have a real chef coming for the weekend."

Noting her awed tone, Jared leaned against the counter. "Do we?"

"Sometimes Lenny's cousin comes in to help with the cookin'—he works at some chain restaurant in the city."

"Lenny?"

"Mrs. Rutherford's chauffeur. More usual, it's me making chicken salad." She paused and sighed. "Or Master Richard fires the grill."

Since Jared had worked for Rose Rutherford several times in the past, he'd gotten a healthy, but not always pleasant, dose of her son, Richard. Wanting to be called "master" while not being one in any way described him entirely. Richard had started Rutherford Securities with his family's money and influence, and at least had the sense to hire people who knew what they were doing. While he'd been busy decorating his office and having power lunches with his country club golfing buddies, the company became a success—heaven knew how.

He'd be eaten alive by a slow-moving, milk-producing cow on any ranch worth a damn.

"Those nights we wind up ordering from a restaurant in town," Mrs. K finished.

"But not this weekend."

"No." Her expression brightened. "Shelby's a caterer in the city, and her supplier brought the most wonderful ingredients. I can't wait to see what she does with them."

"It'll be a barn burner, I'm sure."

Mrs. K swatted his arm. "Oh, go on with ya, Jared dear, I think Mrs. Rutherford was aiming for something more sophisticated. She made it clear she wants the good silver, crystal and china set out each night."

"Uh-huh." Based on the range of high-energy activities he'd been hired to pull off, he thought the guests would be lucky to sit upright at the end of the day, much less enjoy elegant entrées prepared by a city chef. "So this is an adventure weekend for gourmets?"

"You know Master Richard. He likes his appearances."

So why hadn't the Rutherfords plopped a captain at the wheel of their yacht and taken their guests for cocktail-filled rides along the coast?

Because Richard was determined to prove his manhood.

Jared just hoped his insurance rider would cover accident by arrogance.

"I expect gourmets will be all over," Mrs. K said, continuing her unnecessary straightening of the kitchen knick-knacks. "The chef's a friend of Victoria Holmes." She raised her blond-going-gray eyebrows. "Quite the family."

Jared knew the influential Holmes crowd. At the direction of Victoria's mother, Joanne Holmes, and the family's charity foundation staff, he'd once put on a ranch fantasy weekend for a group of their benefactors. Finding the lady cold and distant, he'd put all his effort into giving the city-born teens the country experience of a lifetime.

Despite dealing with the occasional difficult client, however, he loved his business—though he didn't have to work at all. He had assets as solid as his weekend employers'.

But Mrs. K couldn't know about that.

No one save his accountant, his office manager and his immediate family knew he didn't just work at Flaming Arrow Adventure Tours, he owned it.

He'd come to the Rutherford estate for the house party because he genuinely liked Rose, and organizing wild weekends for high-powered executives was as good a challenge as any.

Fighting frustration with city people who looked down on those who worked with their hands had simply become part of the job. His hands, as well as his father's and grandfather's, had made them millionaires many times over. Hard work made the results all the more satisfying.

Maybe that was why Richard annoyed him so much. He always seemed determined to take the easy route.

"Where are Rose and Richard?" he asked the housekeeper.

She scrubbed a spot on the marble counter that Jared couldn't see. "They're gettin' ready for the guests. Mrs. Rutherford had a stylist come out to select all her clothes for the weekend. They should be finished soon."

A stylist who made house calls on holiday weekends and picked out a grown woman's clothes for her as his mother had for him. When he was four. It was a strange, strange world sometimes.

Footsteps sounded on the back stairs, and seconds later Ruthanne, Richard's wife, strolled in. Dressed in a bright floral dress and gold jewelry, and carrying a wide-brimmed straw hat, she radiated youthful energy and was the perfect contrast to her husband's overblown self-importance.

"Isn't it a beautiful day?" she asked.

"Yes, Ms. Ruthie." Mrs. K crossed to the fridge. "I made lemonade this morning. Would you like some?"

She smiled broadly. "How sweet. Yes, thank you."

"The Jet Skis are ready whenever you want to take a ride," Jared said.

"We'll probably wait until after tea." Ruthie accepted an ice-filled glass from Mrs. K. Pausing before taking a sip, she said, "You remember the guests aren't actual daredevils like you."

Jared snapped his fingers. "Damn. There goes my plan to hang glide off the nearest lighthouse."

Lemonade sloshed over the rim of her glass as Ruthane whirled. "Jared, you're not really—"

He held up his hand. "I know how to handle tenderfoots."

"They're not all that delicate," Ruthie said, linking arms with him. "You'll like..." She stopped as she noticed the housekeeper on her hands and knees. "Mrs. Keegan, what are you doing down there?"

"The lemonade, Ms. Ruthie." She rose and tossed the paper towel she held in the trash. "A chef's kitchen should be spotless."

"This kitchen is always spotless, and there's no need to put on airs for my friends." Ruthanne's mouth drew into a thin line. "Though I'm not sure about this last-minute couple my husband invited."

Distracted by the sun's glare through the back window, Jared wished he'd followed his first impulse and laid out on the dock instead of heading for the house. He'd always rather be outside.

"Jared?" Ruthie said, drawing his attention. "You'll like *my* guests. Richard has some business thing going on, as usual, but we're determined not to let the weekend be boring. Who wants to sit around a stuffy old boardroom all day?"

"Some do." He shook his head. "Can't imagine why."

"Naturally, that's where you come in."

"My favorite spot."

Ruthie patted his forearm. "You're looking fit as always. What diet are you on?"

"The Jet Ski riding, hang gliding one."

She sighed, leading him to the small table in the corner of the kitchen. "I have to watch every bite I eat. I must be crazy to invite Shelby out here."

The words were barely out of her mouth before the intercom on the wall buzzed. "Rutherford residence," Mrs. K answered.

"Victoria Holmes, Shelby Dixon and Calla Tucker at the gate to see Ruthanne Rutherford."

Mrs. K pressed a code on the numbered panel. "Yes, we're expecting you. Come up the driveway, please."

While the housekeeper rushed around the kitchen, wiping spotless counters, Jared rattled off the weekend activities for Ruthie. In addition to a small yacht and Jet Skis, the Rutherfords had a powerboat for pulling water skis and inner tubes. He also had scuba diving and fishing trips planned.

"It's Friday, Jared," Ruthie commented. "We're going to do all that before Monday?"

He glanced at his watch. "We could do it all by sunset if you like."

As she shook her head ruefully, the doorbell rang.

"I'll get it," Mrs. K exclaimed, wiping her hands on her apron as she shot out of the kitchen.

"I've never seen her like this," Ruthie said, watching the housekeeper rush down the hall. "It's like a celebrity coming to the house."

Jared hoped the noted chef could cook something hearty. He wasn't much on complicated sauces and names of dishes nobody but a native-born Parisian could pronounce. Personally, he'd enjoy a nice, thick steak.

The hallway was soon filled with female voices, and Jared rose as the group approached the kitchen. A blonde, a brunette and a redhead. How diversified.

Ruthie received hugs; he got curious stares.

At his height—six foot four in bare feet and no boots—he guessed his towering presence was a bit intimidating.

To some, anyway.

He spotted the Holmes heiress immediately. She looked like her mother, but not. Her icy-blue eyes warmed as she talked to her friends, then narrowed when aimed at him. Of the women, she was also the tallest, nearly six feet in the blade-sharp black stiletto heels she wore.

She was stunning, but not his type at all. Cool perfection

wrapped in moneyed NYC sophistication. When Ruthie introduced them, her smile was as distant as a Montana winter.

She extended her hand. "My idea of adventure is a massage at the spa, so I doubt we'll be seeing much of each other this weekend."

As he took her hand, heat slid through his veins, surprising him. There was something about her...something challenging, interesting. He found himself considering ways to thaw her out.

"Your mother didn't like me much when she first met me, either." He smiled as suspicion flitted through Victoria's eyes. "She warmed up eventually."

2

VICTORIA PULLED HER HAND AWAY from Jared McKenna and resisted the urge to make a fist to dispel the tingling sensation
she'd gotten from touching him. "You know my mother?"

"I took her and some teens from the foundation on a cowboy adventure weekend last year."

Victoria remembered her grandmother mentioning the
event, as Nana was determined to get her daughter out of
the city and into a wide-open space. Something about fear
of dust and a lack of vitamin D. Victoria had been thrilled
she hadn't been recruited.

Fear of dust was a documented condition that specifically
targeted people with a mostly black wardrobe.

Victoria raised her eyebrows at the man before her. "My
mother rode a horse?"

"No, but the kids and the staff did, and they loved it, so
she was happy."

How could he tell her mother was happy? Had she actually smiled? Complimented him? Joanne didn't warm up to
people, either.

Even big, hot outdoorsmen.

Especially big, hot outdoorsmen.

He had ridiculously broad shoulders, muscular arms, and
a deep tan that could only come from spending endless hours

in the sun. No lack of vitamin D there. With his wrinkled T-shirt and khaki shorts, bare feet, windblown dark hair and laughing brown eyes, he seemed the antithesis of any man she'd be interested in.

And yet he'd survived a weekend with her mother. If there was anything Victoria admired, it was resiliency.

This guy was the walking, breathing picture of rugged.

"Hi, Ruthanne," Shelby said from beside Victoria. "It's great to finally meet you."

"You, too. And call me Ruthie. Everybody does." Her gaze flicked to Victoria. "Except Vicky, of course."

Victoria clenched her jaw. Her name was not Vicky. She, in fact, hated to be called that—as Ruthanne well knew.

Before she could remind her friend of that detail, Shelby asked a question about her supplies for the weekend, and all the other women followed Mrs. K on her tour of the kitchen and pantry.

"The pantry requires a tour?" Victoria asked, though only Jared was around to hear her.

"They used to have a footman haul stuff the full ten feet from the pantry to the counter, but he wasn't fast enough, so he was let go."

Victoria resisted the urge to smile. The house was certainly like something out of the English countryside, and the perfect setting for formal servants. But clearly, Jared the Rugged wasn't a history major.

"Footmen don't work in the kitchen," she said.

"You'd know."

"How? I live in an apartment in Manhattan. I don't have a footman."

"A maid?"

"I use a cleaning service."

"Every day?"

"Every week." She crossed her arms over her chest. "Is there a particular reason you're interested in my domestic situation?"

That crafty grin appeared. "Long as we're on the subject... do you have a live-in boyfriend?"

"No," Victoria answered, before she thought to tell him her relationships were none of his business.

"Sleepover boyfriend?"

"I don't see how this—"

"Pretty cranky response, so I'd say no. I bet you kick them out fifteen minutes after sex."

"I do *not*."

"After a one-for-the-road drink?"

"No."

She gave her lover a bottle of water before he left. And they all left perfectly satisfied. What was he implying? That she was lousy in bed? That she was cold and methodical like her mother? Not that she knew about her mom in bed, anyway.

In fact, the whole idea of her in the throes of passion seemed wrong.

Maybe Victoria had been fertilized in a petri dish. And why, before now, hadn't she ever thought to ask that question? It made perfect sense. Given her grandfather's proclivity toward science and brilliant surgical techniques, why hadn't she wondered—

Halting her runaway thoughts, it occurred that in less than a minute Jared had more information about her personal life than her assistant had in five years.

Victoria glared at him. "So I guess those muscles in your biceps don't cloud your brain power, do they?"

His eyes softened to a shade of gold. He lifted his arm and flexed the muscle. "You noticed, huh?"

He had to be kidding with this come-on. "Look here, buddy," she said, leaning forward, only to continue in an urgent whisper, "I don't have time for your games. I'm not here to flirt or banter or have sex—which I'm great at, by the way. I'm here to get a promotion. Richard Rutherford's account is going to secure my future. I don't know who you think you're playing—maybe the mealy daughter of the legendary Joanne Holmes—but I'm not her. I've got my own success and agenda, and that's going to take me to the top."

"Do you have any idea how hot you are right now?"

"I…" She stopped, humiliated to realize a heated flush was crawling up her neck. There was no way she was turned on. She was…surprised.

But nobody caught her off guard.

"You need to take a big step backward, cowboy," she said, keeping her voice low and firm.

"*Me?* You're the one who moved closer. You step back."

"I will not."

"So what do you suggest we do, since we're already this close?"

"We're not going to do anything."

"No ideas? Fine." He slid the pad of his thumb across her bottom lip. "I have a few."

"Everybody getting settled in?"

At the sound of Richard Rutherford's voice, Victoria leaped away from Jared.

Her heart pounded against her chest. What was she doing? How could she have forgotten even for a minute her reason for coming to the house party?

She approached Richard as he stood by the kitchen counter. Her professional smile was now in place and all distracting thoughts about Jared McKenna set aside. "Richard, it's so good to see you. What a lovely spot for a weekend party."

"Thank you, Victoria." Wearing a browny-beige-and-yellow argyle sweater and khaki pants, he looked like the picture of Casual Rich Man on Weekend Golf Outing. "We're pleased to have you as our guest."

His formal speech struck her oddly. It was classic Richard, but it was wrong. That damn Jared. His easy, casual manner had spoiled normalcy.

"I know we're all going to have a great time," she said, "but I was hoping we could find a few minutes to talk about the new campaign."

Richard smiled. "I'm sure we will. Business is pleasure, after all."

"Exactly." *That* was normal. How could she have gotten distracted by some barefoot cowboy wannabe? Correction, adventure tour guide. What kind of job was that, anyway?

For romantic liaisons, she had more sophisticated men in mind. For professional pursuits, she had a plan, and she was making it work.

It *had* to work.

The intercom buzzed again. "That's probably our other guests, Mrs. Keegan," Richard announced, as the housekeeper bustled back into the kitchen. "When they get to the house, bring them into the front parlor. We'll have tea there and let everyone get acquainted."

Jared started toward the back door. "I'll make sure all the equipment is ready to go."

"No, no." Richard waved his hand. "Join us for tea. It'll be easier to introduce everyone at the same time."

Jared looked as if he'd rather handle a live rattlesnake.

Victoria had to agree with his foreboding. She couldn't imagine that big body perched on one of Rose's antique settees or holding a dainty china cup.

But the rough-and-tumble Mr. McKenna, thankfully, wasn't Victoria's problem. "Who else is coming?" she asked Richard. "Anybody I know?"

Maybe he'd invited some executives from his company. Wouldn't it be convenient if she got to meet the vice president of operations? Or even marketing? She could impress all the decision makers in one fell swoop and have the contract ready by the time she got back to the office on Tuesday, the day Coleman Sr. announced his retirement. She could almost hear the champagne cork pop.

She was so caught up in her fantasy, she almost didn't catch the name Richard said.

And when she did, she was sure she was hallucinating.

"Did you just say Peter Standish?" she managed to query around the lump in her throat.

He nodded. "And his wife, Emily. Charming couple. They really—"

"I'm sorry." Victoria could hardly believe she was interrupting him, but it was vital she dispel her delusion before anyone noticed she was on the verge of panicking. "Not the same Peter Standish who works at Coleman?"

Richard smiled as if he'd given her a particularly clever gift. "The very same. All one, big, happy family."

Victoria's mouth went dry. "But…"

Calla darted to her side and slid her arm around her waist, obviously noticing that Victoria needed the support. "Richard, would you mind if I took some pictures of the property while I'm here this weekend? I'm hoping to do an article for *Atlantic Magazine*."

"Snap away. In fact, after tea I'll show you where *Beachside Homes* shot their summer spread."

"Oh, would you?" Beaming at him, Calla stepped forward and linked her arm with Richard's. "I want all the details."

Victoria stared, frozen, as they headed out of the room. She could hear Shelby and Mrs. Keegan preparing tea and trays of cookies, but their voices seemed to float to her from a long way off.

"Who's Peter Standish?" Jared asked from close behind her. "One of the lovers you kicked out without so much as a one-for-the-road drink?"

She didn't have the strength for a comeback, or even to move away. In fact, she considered turning around and laying her head against his wide, muscular chest—if only for a second. "My office rival," she said woodenly.

"What do you do?"

She swiveled and wished she hadn't, since their faces—specifically their lips—wound up mere inches apart. "My mother didn't tell you?"

Confusion swam in his eyes. "Not that I remember."

Why would she? She's The Legend; I'm the trainee. "I'm a vice president at Coleman Public Relations."

He straightened, and she was almost sorry for the loss of closeness. "Ah...the new safe."

Victoria scowled. "What do you know about it? It's supposed to be top secret."

"Rose told me."

Victoria found that an odd way for a temporary employee to refer to the venerable Rose Rutherford. But then her hostess had a fair amount of charm, which she was rumored to dispense heavily on cute, young guys.

"You really think you can convince people to spend several grand on a big metal box?" he asked.

My mother could. Dispelling all doubt, Victoria lifted her chin. "Given the right motivation, I can convince people to spend several grand on anything."

"And what's the right motivation this time?"

"The Rutherford Securities contract and a senior vice presidency."

"One the unwelcome Mr. Standish is also up for?"

"Not if my boss has any sense."

"Does he?"

"Most of the time." She fisted her hand at her side. "What is he doing here? Why is he ruining my plans? Why in the world did Richard invite him?"

"Your boss?"

Victoria sighed. Jared had already proved he wasn't dense. Being difficult, however, seemed to come just as naturally. "My rival."

"Want my opinion?"

"You ride horses *and* consult on corporate politics?"

His eyes darkened for an instant, and she knew the insult had hit home. She was unprepared when his reaction made her feel guilty, though.

When had she gotten so mean?

Victoria had never been particularly gentle, but her obsession with ambition had changed her. Tact was rare outside of landing a deal. Vulnerability was reserved for only a few. Was her desire to live up to her mother's legacy so important? Was it really impossible to be successful and yet different from her?

"I watch people," he said, his anger restrained, yet apparent. "Mostly people like you. You run around in circles, chasing each other, or the next big deal or trophies and promotions. Seems to me like a giant waste of time."

What else is there? she almost asked. "And what do you do that's so much better?"

"I chase adventure," he said, his voice quiet and deep. "Wanna join me?"

She dismissed the spark of desire she felt. She had bigger things at stake than sex. And abandoning a lifetime of climbing the corporate ladder wasn't an option. Hell, ambition was coded into her DNA. "Can't," she said, forcing strength into her voice that usually came naturally. "I need this promotion."

"You probably deserve it."

"I do."

"So you surely realize why Richard invited you and your rival to the same party."

"Do I?"

"Yeah. Richard likes to be the center of attention."

"Of course he does, but how do you know—" She stopped as his intention became clear. "Richard wants us to fight for the contract."

Jared nodded.

Victoria wanted to scream over the injustice. If Peter got the Rutherford contract instead of her, he'd likely get the senior VP position, too. Her grand plan was crumbling around her, and all before the weekend had even started.

"If it matters," Jared said lightly, "I'm rooting for you."

"Why?"

He shrugged. "I like winners."

"And you think I'll win."

"Call it a hunch."

3

WHILE THE SUN BURNED invitingly outside, Jared drank tea and learned tons of useless information.

The temperature was ninety-one, the traffic was murder, a local politician had been caught in an illicit affair with his assistant, and Richard and Peter had played golf earlier in the week, which led Rich to tell his buddy about the new safe and the impending PR campaign.

Jared didn't consider chasing a little white ball across manicured lawns an actual sport, but he recognized that more deals were made during such mundane silliness than were negotiated in boardrooms.

Standing in the corner, since he didn't trust the structural integrity of Rose's antique furniture, he bit into a cookie and realized one positive thing—Chef Shelby could cook.

He had no doubt Victoria was mad enough to chew nails, but she held her teacup and smiled indulgently as the golfing buddies recounted their round.

"Are they going to tell us about every stroke on every hole?" he asked Shelby, who had approached him with an offer of more cookies, which he gratefully took.

"Apparently." Watching the pair demonstrate teeing off at hole fifteen, she angled her head, seeming to feel the same confusion Jared did. "Guys at home in Georgia brag about shooting animals in the woods and drinking beer."

"Guys in Montana are pretty much the same."

"Richard isn't really going to hire that goofy suck-up Peter over Victoria, is he?"

"I'm not sure management is his strong suit."

Shelby focused on Jared, obviously suspicious about how a ski and scuba expert understood corporate hiring. "Oh?"

"Not my specialty, either," he said casually. He was going to have to be more careful what he said if he planned to pull off his disguise as a mere employee. "'Course, I've made bad decisions myself. He once talked me into letting him parasail."

"Sounds fun. How was that a bad idea?"

"He's afraid of heights."

"Which he discovered once he was a hundred feet in the air, I'll bet."

Jared winked. "You got it."

"I can't imagine what's keeping Mother," Richard said loudly, dragging Jared's attention back to the rest of the group.

"Oh, gee," Shelby muttered to Jared. "We've already gone through all eighteen holes?"

"Seemed like a lot more."

As Shelby laughed, Victoria glared in Jared's direction. What'd he do? Turncoat Richard got indulgent smiles, and he got the brunt of her temper? How was that fair?

He could use some fresh air. "I'm sure Rose'll be down in a minute," he said to the assembly. "While we're waiting, why don't we head outside? I'll show everybody what we've got planned for the weekend."

Setting their teacups aside, the group followed Jared out of the room.

"I'm not really good with animals," Victoria said as she passed him at the back door.

Richard moved up beside her and slipped his arm around her waist. "Not to worry. The horses are upstate in a show.

Jared has water sports set up—Jet Skis, fishing gear and scuba equipment. Something for everybody."

She fixed her gaze on Jared. "All that, huh?"

He stared right back. "I'll be happy to demonstrate anything you think you might like."

Calla, walking behind Victoria, giggled, clearly getting the double meaning in his offer. Victoria ignored him and picked up her pace down the brick stairs.

She was going to fall and break her neck in those ridiculous shoes.

Before he followed the guests, he noticed Shelby and Mrs. K loading the dishwasher. "Come on, ladies. You, too. You can't stay cooped up in the kitchen for four days."

The housekeeper waggled her finger. "With all you've got goin' on, Jared dear, everybody's got to be properly fed." Nevertheless, the two women followed him out the door.

Once there, Jared took a deep, relieved breath.

Hot though it might be in the sun, he'd been claustrophobic in the house. Crystal blue-green water dotted with whitecaps brushed the pristine sandy shore. Clumps of sea grass bracketed the wooden dock jutting toward the ocean. Boating traffic was fairly light today, though by Saturday afternoon the waterways would be teaming with crafts of every shape and size.

When a man had this kind of view, why waste time looking at anything else?

Not to mention that *kind of view.*

He watched Victoria's backside sway as she strolled onto the dock. Though her hand was tucked around Richard's arm, Jared was confident he'd feel her touch soon enough.

Even out of his element, he had a fair amount of charm. And he couldn't wait to use it to break through the reserved shell around Victoria Holmes.

Whistling, he joined the others on the dock. "Is this everybody?"

"Except Mother," Richard said.

"And her gentleman friend, Sal," Ruthie added. "He's arriving around dinnertime."

Rose had a boyfriend? Good for her. Plus, romance on as many fronts as possible could only help his cause with Victoria.

Especially since, at the moment, she seemed determined to monopolize Richard, for reasons that had nothing to do with passion.

Still, a little moonlight, a good meal, a stroll on the beach… Maybe Jared could get Victoria to set business aside for a while.

"How many of you have ever scuba dived?" he asked the assembled group.

Only Peter's and Victoria's hands went up.

"You don't have to worry about me," her colleague said smugly. "I'm an expert diver."

Victoria pressed her lips together as if resisting the urge to contradict him. "I went on a couple of dives in college, if that counts."

"It does," Jared assured her. "It'll come back to you. For everyone else who's interested, I can teach you the basics in the pool in an hour or so. If you're comfortable, we can go on a short dive. If not, there's plenty of snorkeling equipment to use."

As Jared explained all the activities available, the importance of not doing anything alone, and the tentative schedule he'd worked out, he discovered Peter was apparently an expert at everything. And yet Jared would bet his best saddle the guy didn't know how to swim competently, much less that he'd dived at the Great Barrier Reef.

"Anybody want to hop on a Jet Ski?" he asked to stall Peter's next overblown story.

As he'd expected, nearly everyone refused. He'd discovered city people had to gradually warm up to fun. This crowd would probably walk down the steps of the pool rather than simply dive in.

Calla, his only volunteer, ran up to the house to get her suit on, but the others wanted to unpack and get ready for dinner. Shelby and Mrs. K had to start making the meal.

"Steak?" Jared asked hopefully as he descended the ladder toward the Jet Ski floating there.

"Thai food," Shelby called down. "Fish cakes, grilled pork satay, cucumber salad, baked shrimp with noodles, and chicken curry."

Mrs. K clasped her hands. "Doesn't it sound exotic? Shelby's going to show me how to make everything."

Climbing on the watercraft, Jared saluted. "Based on the cookies, I have full faith in both of you. But is there steak in my future?"

"Monday," they said as one.

"For future reference," Shelby added with a wink, "Victoria loves Thai food."

Jared had no doubt she did. Exotic and spicy fit her perfectly.

He started the engine, then glanced up to spot Richard walking toward the house with Peter on one side and Victoria on the other.

Why the image bothered him so much, Jared wasn't sure.

Instead, he focused on his job. He helped Calla onto the Jet Ski, and she held on for dear life as he streaked through the waves, jumped the crests and turned his face to the sun and salty spray.

The vision of Victoria's stunning face wouldn't go away, however. He compared the blue of the sea to her eyes. He remembered the startling black sand of Waianapanapa Beach in Maui, and how her hair would blend into it like an ancient exotic goddess merging with the land. He wondered how she'd fare on the open waters, unconstrained by obligations and ambition.

Calla had no such restraints and soon was ready to take the controls of the craft herself. Jared stood on the shore, watching to be sure she didn't run into trouble, and wondering why the buxom blonde didn't move him the way her friend did.

In all his travels, he'd learned some bits of truth. Don't grab live stone crabs without gloves or a high pain threshold. Don't hang glide with anybody after three cocktails. Don't trust an African tribal guide who says crocodiles are "babies at heart."

To that knowledge he'd add that chemistry wasn't always a definable concept.

Calla was delightful. But Victoria was trapped in her orderly, fluorescent-light world, and he desperately wanted to release her.

"Any chance of getting Victoria on a Jet Ski?" he asked her friend after he tied off the machine and they'd climbed back onto the dock.

Calla's gaze met his before quickly skittering away. "I don't see how."

"She's here on business, not fun."

"As always."

"What kind of men does she date?"

Calla's steps faltered, as if she hadn't expected him to be so direct, but she recovered quickly. "Jerks," she muttered with a shrug.

"Jerks?" he repeated, as if that was music to his ears.

"Rich jerks." She waved her hand. "Oh, they all have great hair and pretty faces, successful careers, 401Ks and portfolios. But they're superficial and—" She clamped her hand over her mouth. "I can't believe I just said that." She broke into a brisk stride.

He caught up to her, bringing her to a stop. "Sorry. I shouldn't have asked."

"I shouldn't have answered."

"We had a…moment earlier." He wasn't sure that was the way to describe the intensity of the spark that had ignited the instant Victoria had touched him, but that was all he had. "I was only wondering if she'd be interested in some-body like me."

Calla grinned. "You like her."

"Oh, yeah."

Calla's gaze trailed over him. "Great hair and pretty face, check."

When she paused, he finished her thought. "But a 401K and portfolio, not so much."

"You don't have either, I guess?"

He did. But why should that matter? Why did it *always* matter? "Do I need them?"

Calla frowned, and he knew she was thinking of a way to let him down gently, to tell him that Victoria was particular and, being a successful woman herself, only hung out with guys who moved in her same circle.

He could move in those circles. He simply chose not to.

Too much artifice. Too many hangers-on. Too many peo-ple who clung because he had the means to buy a round for the house.

Been there. College in L.A. had schooled him in more ways than business management.

"She needs a regular guy," Calla announced to Jared's sur-prise. "Clearly, her pattern of brief relationships with shallow men isn't working out. And if she ever stops focusing on her career twenty-four hours a day, she'll see that."

"Would she really? I'm a regular guy," Jared said confi-dently, since he was—sort of.

Calla widened her eyes in mock surprise. "Are you? What an amazing coincidence." She winked. "You two could make a great couple." She jogged toward the house, calling her thanks as she left him.

Smiling, Jared turned for the shore. He hadn't expected details from Victoria's friend, especially since he'd had no right to ask about her love life in the first place.

Rich jerks who don't hang around long, huh?

Good thing he usually concealed his ownership of the

company. His clients thought he simply worked for the firm, same went for the host and guests this weekend.

One regular guy at your service, Ms. Holmes.

TWO HOURS LATER, DRESSED FOR dinner, but still missing her usual confidence, Victoria strode into the kitchen. "I need a martini, stat."

While Shelby continued to chop vegetables, Calla jumped off the counter where she'd been sitting and headed to the fridge. From the freezer side, she pulled out a filled and frosted glass. Two extra-large olives speared on a toothpick floated inside the liquid.

Calla handed over the drink. "We figured you'd come asking for this."

Victoria took a grateful sip, the harsh bite of the olives and liquor suiting her sour mood perfectly. "Where's Mrs. Keegan?"

"In the wine cellar," Shelby said. "So vent away."

"What the hell does Richard think he's doing?" Victoria asked her friends.

"Haven't got a clue," Calla answered, returning to her perch on the counter.

Shelby dumped chopped celery into a mixing bowl. "It's got to be some kind of ego thing. Like having two dates to the prom."

"Why would you want to have two dates to the prom?" Calla asked.

"*I* wouldn't." Shelby shrugged. "But some people would."

"This is business," Victoria reminded them. "Not social hour. And highly unprofessional."

Calla shook her head. "Shelby's got a point. There's nothing technically wrong with it, apart from being underhanded and sneaky. But that's business as usual for you."

"He invites me and my friends for a relaxing weekend, tells me about his supposedly top secret new safe, then asks my competition to tag along and work directly against me for his contract. How do you figure that's business as usual?"

"It's like an on-the-job interview," Calla said, her tone matter-of-fact. "Obviously, Coleman's retirement isn't the big secret you thought it was, and Richard wants to pick the best person to replace him for the ad campaign."

Victoria contemplated the remaining contents of her glass and wondered if downing it in one swallow would make her look as desperate as she felt. "Thanks for your support, best friend."

Calla sighed. "You have my support, as always."

"Come on, hon," Shelby added. "A competition between you and Peter hardly seems fair. Maybe you should spot him ten points or something."

"Let's not go that far," Calla said. "Didn't you hear him bragging earlier? The sooner he gets knocked out in this bout, the happier we'll all be. And you…" She waggled her finger at Victoria. "We're not happy about what Richard did, but you have to admit it makes sense. Frankly, it seems like something you'd do."

Victoria's jaw dropped. "Take that back."

"Since when did you get so thin-skinned?" Calla asked.

"Since my mother called me and wanted to know why I hadn't been promoted yet. And did I realize she'd been the youngest senior VP in the history of the company, and did I know I hadn't met that goal, and did I want her to call Coleman Sr. and *put in a good word.*"

Silence fell.

Calla's face went red, and Shelby paused her dinner prep. "When did this happen?" Shelby asked gently.

"A few days ago." Victoria was already regretting her outburst. She wanted to earn her promotions. Wanted to be a success without her mother's help. "Same old, same old. I don't know why I let her get to me." Victoria waved her hand in dismissal. She would never live up to The Legend. But, damn, she wanted to make a respectable race out of it. "How was the Jet Ski?"

Calla smiled widely. "That is one hot cowboy."

The spurt of jealousy that shot through Victoria caught her off guard. "I thought you were crazy about Detective Antonio."

"I am sometimes," Calla said, "but he's mad at me right now."

"Why?" As far as Victoria had been able to tell, the attraction went both ways.

Calla rolled her eyes. "Who knows? He's as ornery as a wet cat." Looking smug, she added, "Anyway, Jared's interested in somebody besides me."

Victoria sipped her drink and said nothing.

"I'm with Calla on this one," Shelby stated. "There's no way you haven't noticed, V."

"Does anybody else think it's ironic for Richard to be trolling for PR executives for a safe campaign, while at the same time hiring Mr. Adventure to keep us running around like deranged daredevils?"

Clearly not deterred by Victoria's attempt to change the subject, Calla slid off the counter and moved toward her. "Come on. Don't you think he's cute?"

"No," Victoria returned, completely honest. Cute was nowhere in the same hemisphere with Jared McKenna.

Strong, capable and smokin' hot? Absolutely.

Finishing her martini, she set the glass on the counter. "I'm leaving now. Thanks for the drink."

"You like him," Calla insisted, blocking her exit.

Victoria scooted around her friend. "What is this—middle school?"

"We were all silly girls once," Calla called after her.

Though she paused in the doorway, Victoria didn't turn back. "I wasn't."

Rolling her shoulders, she moved down the hall to the stairs. The house boasted a variety of decks and sunrooms, and Victoria was intent on reaching the one outside the third-floor game room.

She really wished she could give in to her friends' light mood, and before Peter had shown up and spoiled her weekend—along with the near certainty of her promotion—she might have. Now, however, the stakes had been raised, she was knocked off balance and she had to get her stance back in a hurry, or she'd be the one lying on the mat.

As she stepped through the French doors and onto the balcony, she was glad she'd changed into a sleeveless blue dress. The summer heat showed no sign of abating.

But the crashing waves against the shore helped her state of mind and reminded her of her own strength. Even with the complication of her rival, she'd find a way to win Richard's business. Failure wasn't an option.

"I'm not sure I could ever get used to that view."

Nearly jumping out of her skin, she whirled.

Jared was stretched out on a lounge chair, a beer bottle in his hand. As he rose, the long, strong length of him towering over her, she took a second to calm her runaway pulse, as well as notice he'd changed clothes. A perfectly pressed white dress shirt covered his broad chest, and the tips of scuffed brown boots peeked from beneath his dark jeans.

"I didn't realize anybody was up here," she said, resisting the urge to lick her lips as a breeze ruffled his dark hair and warmth rose in his brown eyes. Why did he have to be so damn appealing?

"Since you didn't immediately scowl at me, I kinda figured that."

"I don't scowl at you every minute."

"Most minutes." Setting his beer aside, he joined her at the railing, resting his forearms against the wood. "Calla and I missed you on the Jet Skis earlier."

"I had my hair and nails done this morning. I didn't realize Richard was planning Water Weekend Adventures from

Hell. Do you have any idea what a blowout at a top Manhattan salon costs?"

"Nope."

"And you don't care."

"Nope. But I bet your hair and nails are always perfect."

"They are. Is there something wrong with a professional appearance?"

"Not when you're being professional, I guess. But I think—and maybe this is just me—you'd look great messed up."

"Messed up?"

"Maybe mussed up." He leaned close. "You know, tousled, disheveled…" He stroked her cheek with the tip of his finger. "Thoroughly pleasured."

Heat raced through her body. "Are you always this forward with women you've just met?"

He grinned. "Not always."

Despite her earlier anxiety, she found herself smiling back. "Most of the time, I bet you are."

She wished she could find a reason to step away from him and not give in to his touch.

How about your potential contract? Your job? Your promotion? Simple common sense?

For once she ignored the warning from her conscience. "Did my mother really warm up to you?"

"Nope."

"So why did you say she did?"

"I was flirting with you."

Victoria laid her palm on his chest. "You aren't my type."

"You're not mine, either."

But he wrapped his arm around her and kissed her anyway.

4

WITH HIS HANDS FULL OF THE elegant and volatile Victoria, Jared fought to keep his touch soft. Being tentative wasn't really in his nature, but though his instinct was to press her against the nearest wall and ravage her like some randy cowboy who'd ridden the range for far too long, he didn't think that impulse would fly.

He pulled her close, and angling his head, slid his tongue past her lips. He kept his moves slow, steady…enticing. She let a low moan escape, and desire shot through him as if he'd touched a live wire.

He moved his hands down to her hips, holding her against his erection. The pressure felt both amazing and frustrating.

Breathing hard, she jerked back.

He'd pushed too hard, too fast. Shoving his hands in his back pockets, he grappled for composure. *Hell.*

"I'm sorry," she said, her voice strained. "I shouldn't have—"

He held up his hands. "I made the first move."

"I wanted you to." Clearly regretful, she shook her head. Her perfect, creamy skin was flushed. Her crystal blue eyes reflected confusion. "We have nothing in common."

His gaze met hers. "No, I'd say we have exactly one thing in common."

She didn't flinch. He hadn't expected her to. "I guess we do."

He licked his lips and tasted cotton candy. His palms tingled with the need to touch her again.

"It's my lip gloss," she said, obviously realizing the nature of his struggle. "It's flavored."

"Like candy? I would've laid money on you preferring steak au poivre."

"Meat-flavored lip gloss?"

"Right." He reconsidered. Obviously, he had steak on his mind. Or his stomach. "Champagne?"

She gave him her first genuine smile. "That's more like it."

He extended his hand, which she took. "I bet we can find you some in this palace."

"That's an adventure I can get excited about."

They headed downstairs, and though she let go of his hand when they reached the ground floor, he felt they'd crossed a bridge together. He wouldn't have bet cotton candy and smiles could come with a single kiss, but he figured if he was going to pursue this attraction—and he was—he ought to get used to surprises.

In the parlor, most of the other guests were assembled for the cocktail hour.

The men, with the exception of Peter, were drinking whiskey, while the women, plus Peter, enjoyed champagne. Jared and Victoria exchanged a knowing glance, but he otherwise kept his distance.

This contract was important to her, and he wasn't going to be the one to spoil her plans.

Especially since he had his own ideas for her. And them.

Bottled-up stress required a release, after all. He'd be happy to provide her plenty of physical activity to burn off the tension. A Jet Ski or boat-related outing would do her wonders.

Rose, as she was famous for, made a dramatic entrance. Wearing a peacock-blue silk gown, completely overdone for both the season and the occasion, she swept into the parlor when everyone was half into their drinks and Mrs. K had already brought a round of hors d'oeuvres.

"I'm so sorry to be late," Rose said breathlessly. "I couldn't seem to get my hair to do anything tonight."

Her deep red hair was perfect, as always. But trouble with her style wasn't likely to be the main topic of conversation, since around her neck lay a stunning diamond-and-sapphire necklace. The fathomless blue center stone was octagonal-shaped and easily the size of an egg.

As the women stared—Peter's wife, Emily, let out an actual gasp—Richard smiled indulgently at his mother's antics and poured her a glass of champagne.

"You're not the last to arrive, Mother," he said, handing her the cut crystal. "Sal isn't here yet."

Rose's pink-painted mouth moved into a pout. "I can't imagine what's keeping him."

"He's probably looking for his sunglasses," Ruthie said in an uncharacteristic show of bitchiness.

The necklace *was* a bit blinding.

Richard quickly covered his wife's gaffe by introducing Rose to her guests. Jared got a flirty smile, which he was used to with Rose. He wondered if boyfriend Sal, who could be anywhere from twenty to eighty, given Rose's predilections, was the possessive type.

"I trust you have everything you need to give my guests an unforgettable weekend?" she asked.

"I do." Jared brushed his lips across her powdered cheek. "But you'll be the one who's remembered."

"Jared," Peter said, his tone teasing, "you can't have the keys to the boats *and* the full attention of our beautiful hostess."

More smoothly than Jared would have previously given him credit for, the executive led Rose to a settee and launched into a string of compliments about the estate.

Having already become buddy-buddy with Richard on the

golf course, apparently the PR man had decided to move on to bigger, more powerful prey. It was a smart choice. Richard was certainly a momma's boy. If Rose preferred Peter over Victoria, the Rutherford Securities contract would go to him.

Victoria didn't miss a beat and positioned herself next to Richard. "Is it rude to talk about business before dinner?"

"Not if that's what you want to do," he said graciously. Bracketed between his wife and the stunning Victoria, he seemed, in fact, more than pleased. He directed a wink at Calla. "I assume we can count on your discretion about our developing products and strategies."

"I'm a reporter at heart," she said in her twanging Texas accent. "I know how to protect my sources."

With three women focused on him, and Jared as a standby to impress, Richard gave a description of his new safe. The words *state-of-the-art* were used five times and *breakthrough technology* no less than three. "The digital control panel can be configured for your own four-digit code, voice print or, on the superior model, a retina scan. It's breakthrough technology."

Okay, four.

"Fascinating," Victoria said, looking for all the world as if she believed it.

"Interesting" was Calla's neutral response, just before she shot her friend a questioning look and took a sip of champagne.

Ruthie smiled indulgently at her husband. "Isn't he clever?"

Actually, a team of engineers and computer techs were clever.

Twenty years ago.

The whole fawning business turned Jared's stomach. Because one of the fawners was the woman he wanted? Probably.

But not completely.

Jared's conscience warned him to sip his whiskey and say nothing. But he couldn't keep his reservations to himself. Victoria would probably wind up promoting this flawed product.

"Don't many governments, including our own, already use codes with much higher numbers than four, plus voice prints and retina scans for access to sensitive rooms and data?"

"Perhaps," Richard admitted. "Not that they're willing to share the technology behind their developments. The area of personal security is largely ignored for higher purposes. It's time we take back control of our own lives and valuables. My safe will allow the common man to dictate his own destiny."

Why would he need a PR firm? It seemed obvious Richard could orchestrate his own publicity just fine.

"I wasn't aware of your interest in security, Jared," Richard added with a smug smile. "You know something about codes, voice prints and retina scans?"

"Sure. I've watched a spy movie in the last decade."

Victoria scowled; Calla covered up a laugh with a cough.

"Fiction," Ruthie reminded him. "Who takes that seriously?"

"People don't trust banks. Or the government." Richard held tight to his glass, his annoyance obvious by his white-knuckled grip. "We're giving them another option."

"I think it's a brilliant idea for the times," Victoria said, her gaze shifting to Jared's long enough to deliver a warning glare. Richard, naturally, got a dazzling smile. "It'll be the next big thing. Tell him about the ability to change the code remotely with a mobile device."

"If the security is compromised for any reason," Richard began, "an alarm will sound on the mobile device you choose, allowing you to either change your code or lock down the safe."

"Compromising the security of a safe involves opening the door," Jared pointed out. "By the time you punch in the new code, the thief's already run off with your valuables."

Their host looked smug. "The alarm begins with the first incorrect number pressed on the keypad."

"What if the safe owner presses the wrong number?" he asked.

"Then obviously he or she will ignore the warning alarm," Richard said easily.

"Plus the code's only four numbers," Jared reminded him. "By the time you get the signal and reconfigure—even if you're holding your precious mobile device next to your ear at the time—the thief's already inside."

"It works," Richard insisted. "I've seen it."

Victoria laid her hand on his shoulder. "Of course it does."

The woman who had vibrated at Jared's touch, whose lips had moaned for his kiss mere minutes ago, was focused totally on Richard. The contract. Winning.

Maybe he'd been kidding himself about her response, about the need they shared. "Sorry." He gave his host a curt nod. The security might work, and perhaps Richard was explaining the technology wrong—not surprising, actually. "My bad. I need some air. I'll see all of you at dinner."

Jared strode down the hall, through the kitchen and out the back door. If Victoria wanted to play Richard's game, she was welcome to it. He wanted a different kind of adventure.

DINNER WAS DELICIOUS. If only the conversation surrounding the meal could measure up.

Victoria needed a much sharper knife than the sterling silver one beside her to cut the underlying tension.

Richard maintained his role as charming host, Ruthie relaxed her criticism of her mother-in-law and Rose soaked up everyone's praise. But they also tiptoed around the obvious minefield of Victoria and Peter being office rivals and fighting for the same contract—the one controlled by the charming host.

Plus, Victoria could practically see waves of resentment rolling off Jared, like a tsunami destined specifically for her.

Getting the safe to work was the engineers' problem. She just had to convince people to buy the damn thing. And why Jared cared a whit about quality control at Rutherford Securities, she had no idea. He and Richard seemed determined to be at odds with each other.

She shouldn't be surprised. In her experience, different types often disagreed.

Richard was upper-crust Southampton; Jared was humble Western cowboy.

And why the latter suddenly had such great appeal, she had no idea. Though, as much as she loved her job, she had to admit that lately she'd found unexpected pleasure in attending her family's charity events, reminding her that some people were still genuinely surprised by kindness. Victoria spent most of her waking hours in boardrooms. It was the only life she knew. But seeing her hard work benefit somebody besides her financial advisor and her own ego was refreshing.

Sal Colombo, Rose's gentleman friend, was charming, affluent and genuine. Unlike the men she'd dated, success didn't always translate to an overblown ego. In her fierce drive to the top, she'd somehow forgotten that.

"The pork is excellent," David Greggory, Sal's personal assistant, said, bringing Victoria back to the dinner conversation. "I wonder what spices the chef used."

"Knowing Shelby, something handmade by Italian nuns."

Sitting next to her, David frowned. "Nuns are great cooks? Maybe I should have gone to church more often."

Victoria blinked. Humor was largely lost on this gathering. David was clearly witty as well as efficient. About thirty years old, he had blond hair, a plain face and wasn't wildly attractive, but was dressed impeccably in a charcoal suit, which made her certain he knew his way around uptown Manhattan.

"How long have you been with Sal?" she asked him.

"Six months. I worked in the city for years and was burning out fast."

Victoria nodded. Though she thrived on the energy there, she knew others who didn't. The pace could be brutal.

"I decided to change course," David continued. "Now the

most challenging feat I accomplish is managing Sal's social calendar. It's heaven."

Victoria would go nuts in thirty seconds. But David looked tanned and content, so it must be working for him. He'd consulted with Rose on the decorations for the grand Sunday night party, and since he'd found himself at loose ends for the weekend, he'd been included among the houseguests at the last minute.

Rose laughed just then, drawing Victoria's attention. Jared was leaning close, obviously the source of amusement. How nice.

If only she didn't have to look across the table at his handsome profile, she could remember she wasn't here for hot kisses and moonlit nights. She was here to get a contract.

But the man was a serious pleasure to have in her sights.

Rose laid her hand alongside Jared's rugged jaw as she spoke to him, and his smile flashed.

Okay, maybe Victoria was a little jealous.

While Mrs. K cleared the dishes, Sal settled back in his chair with a satisfied smile. "You should tell your guests about the history of your necklace, my dear." His pale blue eyes sparkled. "It's quite a tale."

"Well…" Rose gestured with her right hand, the middle finger of which was dominated by what had to be at least a seven caret yellow diamond. "Sal is right, as always. First off, it's rumored to be cursed by jealousy."

Peter froze with his lips against his water goblet. Victoria's gaze flicked to Jared before returning to Rose. And Emily's attention shot to her husband's profile.

Not that anybody at this table would know anything about jealousy.

With that thought, Victoria recalled the adventure she and her friends had embarked on in the spring, project Robin Hood.

Shelby's parents had been the victims of a retirement swindle. And with the cops not taking a serious interest in the case, the three friends had boldly taken the law into their own hands and gotten justice for those they loved.

As it turned out, envy had had a starring role in this latest tale, as well.

Tracing the edge of the diamond-encircled sapphire, Rose continued her story. "The sapphire is 99 carats and was mined in Sri Lanka in the 1920s. The diamonds were added by an expert jeweler and set into a necklace for Olivia Howinger, a famous European actress of the day. Her beauty drove men to madness. Alabaster skin, radiant blue eyes, and of course, she was a redhead." Rose patted her own auburn curls. "But the man who finally captured her heart was a hotheaded Italian count. Unfortunately for both of them, the attention Olivia received from men didn't end at her marriage. They continued to send her flowers and gifts, flirt with her at parties and restaurants. The count was beside himself with jealousy and determined to make himself the sole focus of his wife's attention.

"So he had the necklace commissioned and presented to her on her birthday. Which only served to bring more attention to Olivia. One night, he walked into a busy French restaurant, expecting to see his wife waiting for him at their favorite table, only to find another man in his seat. The count shot them both on the spot."

"How horrible," Emily whispered, as if the scene were playing out before them.

"In a delicious way," Rose said, winking. "The necklace was sold at the auction of the count's estate after he was hanged, and ever since, it's inspired envy and possessiveness in all who've laid eyes on its flawless beauty."

Calla, Sal and Peter clapped. David shifted in his seat. Victoria's gaze found Jared's, and the heat between them surged briefly, before he glanced away again. They weren't compatible in the least, she reminded herself, and the sooner she accepted that, the easier this weekend would be.

"Bravo, darling," Sal said, patting Rose's hand.

Though it was an engaging story, real people had died. It seemed incredible that a single woman or a sparkling blue rock could cause so much suffering, but kingdoms had risen and fallen for less.

And while Victoria loved pretty things and had her share of sparkles, she couldn't understand wanting to own something with such a bloody history. Rose was an entirely different kind of woman.

Notorious is as notorious does.

"Thankfully, she has a foolproof safe to keep the gems out of greedy hands," Richard said, his expression smug.

Rose smiled indulgently at her son. "What would I do without you, dear?"

For a second, Ruthie looked as though she might suggest something—and not a nice something—but then she pushed back her chair. "Why don't we have coffee and dessert in the sunroom? The sunset is lovely from there."

As they all walked toward the back of the house, Victoria found herself behind Jared and Calla. "Quite a story," her friend said to him.

"It'd make a nice sidebar to your magazine piece," he suggested, angling his face toward her.

When had they discussed Calla's article? During the Jet Ski ride Victoria wasn't interested in so she wouldn't mess up her hair? Why did that suddenly seem stupid and superficial? And why did he and Calla have to look so lovely together?

Calla shook her head. "I doubt Rose would let me take pictures for publication. I sure wouldn't want everybody to know I owned something so valuable."

"I doubt Rose will care," Jared said. "She's got a foolproof safe, after all."

When Calla laughed, Victoria took the opportunity to move around the two and make her way out to the patio, where she pretended to concentrate on the sunset.

She couldn't possibly be jealous of her friend, any more than she had been of Rose during dinner. Victoria didn't work herself up into a lather about men. And she certainly didn't care who Jared spoke to, flirted with, or anything else.

Her attraction to him was an anomaly. Any woman would be fascinated by him. But Victoria didn't generally follow the crowd. She'd always forged her own path, no matter how hard it might seem.

That damn necklace probably was cursed by jealousy. Had to be. Why else was she fuming in the middle of a magnificent sunset?

She should be with Richard, regaling him with her brilliant ideas for the campaign. In fact…was there a way to convince him and Rose to use the necklace in print ads? *I trust my son with my most valuable possessions. Shouldn't you?*

Cute and sweet, but with the added hits of scandal and class.

It was a possibility. Or at least a place to start.

Cheered, she joined everyone else in the sunroom in time to hear Jared suggest a boat ride after dessert. All the guests agreed, and Ruthie insisted Mrs. K and Shelby come along, as well.

On the way to the dock where the small yacht was anchored, several people complimented Shelby and the housekeeper on the delicious meal. Mrs. K beamed, and Shelby accepted the comments with her usual modest professionalism. Victoria felt certain that even if this weekend did nothing for her or Calla, Shelby would gain new bookings.

With the sun's heat fading, and a breeze kicked up by the elegant boat cutting through the waves, the night had turned divine.

Victoria stood at the stern, watching the wake chop the sea to a frothy tower of white. How long had it been since she'd let her hair tangle as salty wind whipped against her skin?

Her parents had a place near Rose's. She rarely came out. She was too busy working, making contacts, bustling around the city. No wonder Jared enjoyed his job so much.

Not that she'd trade her future corner office for a faceful of sea spray, but she could understand the appeal.

"Hi, sweetie," Shelby said as she slid her arm around Victoria's waist. "Catching a wave?"

Victoria extended her hand over the side of the boat, felt the cool sprinkle of droplets. "Nearly."

Calla bracketed Victoria on the other side. "Any chance we're going to get you more than fingertip deep in that water?"

"Yeah." Victoria tucked her blowing hair behind her ears so she could see her friends. "I might dangle my feet."

"In the pool," Calla added, clearly skeptical.

Shelby smirked. "Wearing a big hat and a heavy layer of sunscreen."

"You're dissing sunscreen?" Victoria asked.

"No way," Shelby said.

Calla grinned. "Provided the tough, tanned and broad-shouldered Jared McKenna doesn't use it all up."

Shelby's eyes lit with interest. "He's quite something, isn't he?"

"I was finally in a good mood, I really was," Victoria lamented, then pointed at Shelby. "And you have a man. Stop lusting after…" She stopped, bit back a curse.

Fighting the wind, Calla wrangled her long blond locks into a ponytail. "After yours?"

"Jared isn't mine," Victoria insisted.

Calla leaned in. "But he could be."

Despite herself, Victoria was curious how Calla had gleaned that information. "How do you know?"

"I've got eyes," she said a little too casually. "I see him staring at you."

"And you looking back," Shelby stated.

The last time her pals had those determined expressions on their faces, Victoria had found herself neck-deep in an undercover sting operation against an unscrupulous retirement-fund swindler. "Are you two going to bug me about this guy all weekend?"

"Yes," they answered together.

"Fine, then. I like him." Facing her friends, Victoria was careful to keep her voice brisk and not allow her imagination to provide visual aids of the man in question. "He's smart, strong-willed, resilient and irritating."

"And gorgeous," Calla added, poking Victoria's arm.

"I've got eyes." Victoria narrowed hers. "I can see that."

"How's he irritating?" Shelby asked. "I think he's charming."

"He's...*challenging,*" Victoria returned, deciding that was the right word to describe the alternating highs of attraction and lows of annoyance she felt in Jared's presence.

"You like challenges." Calla's attention flicked to a point over Victoria's shoulder. "Don't you?" she asked, her voice louder.

What was with her? "Sure, but..." Victoria glanced behind her.

Where Jared stood.

Her heart stopped—and not just because she was curious about who might be steering the boat. "How long have you been there?"

He looked thoughtful. "Let me think...." Then he gave her a broad smile. "You like me."

Victoria whirled to her friends and hoped her glare scorched them on the spot.

5

AFTER ATTEMPTING TO CONVINCE Jared she'd been talking about a guy from work, and absolutely not him, Victoria had focused on the horizon, refusing to speak to her so-called friends, and grinding her back teeth.

Returning to the house after they docked, she retreated to the third-floor balcony to breathe a sigh of relief in private.

Shelby was happily hooked up with her elegant Brit lover; Calla had her attraction to a darkly intense cop. Did they think Victoria wouldn't be satisfied until she had a man in her life, too?

Well, that was crap.

She was perfectly happy working, shopping, dating here and there and hanging with her friends—though, clearly, she was going to have to find new ones after that sneaky move her old ones had pulled.

She'd have to put that on her to-do list. Unfortunately, she didn't have her phone with her, as she'd left it in her room before the boat ride.

Fine. Her brain was still sharp enough to make mental notes.

Even if she was interested in a weekend fling, Jared McKenna wouldn't make the cut. Hot as he might be, she always went for guys with cachet and success. Tour guide wasn't exactly her usual choice of date. Of course, she didn't have much to show for her past relationships, either, and there was something about him that—

She heard the door open and, turning, wasn't surprised to see Jared strolling toward her. "Is this going to be a thing with us?" she snapped.

"Depends on what you mean by thing," he said calmly in the face of her anger.

They could be a lot of things, she supposed, but she chose to ignore the possibilities for intimacy and focus on the immediate conflict.

"A habit," she clarified. "One of us comes out here to be alone, and the other one invades."

Joining her at the railing, he raised his eyebrows. "Invades?"

She was still both embarrassed and vaguely mad. Not a good combination. She made an effort to shrug off both. Emotions wouldn't get her the contract she needed. "Argumentative, as my father would say in court. Sorry," she added.

"Understandable. You've had quite a day."

"Yeah." With the incident on the boat fresh in her mind, she'd almost forgotten about the rest of the lousy afternoon. She stared over the water at the moon and was glad the glowing orb was the only light source. With Jared merely a shadow in the dark, she found it easier to admit the truth. "Things didn't go exactly the way I planned."

"Not too sporting of Richard to spring Peter on you without a heads-up."

"No."

Jared's warmth, the scent of the sea and a hint of fresh, alluring cologne emanated from him. Had he gone to his room to shower before seeking her out? The unexpected. Maybe that was what made him so appealing.

She wasn't a woman who played games with men she was attracted to, and though she should be focused on her job, she wasn't desperate enough to lie to him or herself.

She turned toward him, intending to admit just that, when he asked, "Why the hell are you placating that dumb-ass?"

"Richard?" She'd sensed tension between them, but Jared's outright hostility was revealing. "Fine way to talk about your boss."

"I don't work for him," he said shortly. "Rose hired me."

"Uh-huh." The doting between the two, the secret smiles... Pieces fell into place and formed a picture Victoria didn't particularly relish. "Did you take her on a cowboy adventure weekend, too?"

"No."

"She's an avid Jet Ski rider?"

His lips flipped up at the corners. "She doesn't like to get her hair wet."

"Yet you seem awfully familiar with each other."

"I've worked for her several—" He stopped, his expression speculative. "Are you asking me if I've slept with Rose Rutherford?"

"I am."

He laughed. He pulled Victoria into his arms and laughed harder.

While she was glad he didn't seem angry anymore, and enjoyed the joyous rumbling in his chest, she couldn't help feeling foolish about Rose.

"She's thirty years older than me," Jared said when he'd recovered enough to speak.

"So?" Victoria leaned back to eye him closely. "That's never stopped her before."

"I imagine not." Jared traced his finger along her jaw. "Rose and I aren't, and have never been, lovers."

"Okay." Rose appreciated a hot young guy more than most women her age, a fact Victoria should probably warn Jared about, but she had bigger topics to explore. "Why were you so angry with Richard—and apparently me—earlier? When you stormed out of the cocktail hour?"

"I don't like seeing you fawn over him."

Typically blunt. Something they had in common. "Why?"

His arm tightened around her waist. "I want you to fawn over me."

Her breathing hitched. Her brain buzzed. And she certainly couldn't remember why she'd been so determined to keep him at a distance. "I can do that."

"So why'd you lie earlier about liking me? For the last two hours, I've had visions of some guy you work with showing up to challenge me to a duel."

"I don't…" She angled her head. "A duel?"

"Maybe a shoot-out. You keep callin' me a cowboy."

"Fair enough."

"You still lied," he reminded her.

"I tried to make you believe otherwise, because I don't like to give anybody the upper hand."

"But with me you don't have to live up to some ridiculously impossible ideal."

He'd met her only a few hours ago and already knew her hot-button issue. No way was she that transparent. In his business, she assumed, he had to be sensitive about knowing who was serious about jumping off cliffs and who only wanted to imagine or talk about doing so. But his perception was still unnerving.

"Who do you think's on top when your parents are in bed together?"

She gaped at him. "You're crazy."

"I'm fun." He leaned close. "Wanna see?"

The temptation to tell everybody to go to hell—her friends, her boss, Richard, her parents and especially her own ego—was irresistible.

Jared McKenna…well, she didn't want him to move an inch.

She pressed her lips directly to the pulse beating fast and strong beneath his ear. Pounding for her. "Why not?"

JARED KNEW HIS IDEA OF FUN—which took place in the game room—caught Victoria off guard.

He kicked her butt in air hockey and pinball, but she finessed him at pool. Stone-cold nerves. Some might say her personality mimicked her style behind the cue.

Once, he would have agreed.

But whether by circumstance, luck or fate, he'd seen a vulnerable side of her. A side he wanted to explore, layer by layer.

He also found her clever, determined, ambitious and intensely desirable.

When she again won the match with a sharply banked shot, he leaned against his cue stick and shook his head in disbelief. "That's it. You have to teach me. I could retire to Monte Carlo with a move like that."

Looking more relaxed than he'd seen her during the entire span of their short association, she crooked her finger in his direction. "Come on, big guy."

His heart launched into a gallop at the expression on her face, and when he reached her side, all thoughts of pool vaporized. Even though she wasn't a short woman, she was barefoot, so the top of her head barely reached his chin. Her lithe body made his seem more powerful, and he found himself wrestling with the crazy vision of scooping her into his arms and carrying her off to the nearest bedroom.

He'd probably get his face smacked, but that didn't dispel the romantic idea.

"Yes, ma'am?"

She tilted her head back, her ice-blue eyes full of speculation. "I like that you're tall."

"Do you?"

"In heels, I tower over most men."

"You're not wearing any now."

She glanced down at her feet, wriggling her toes. "So I see. We've known each other seven hours, and I'm already partly naked."

"I'd be happy to help your condition spread."

"I thought you wanted to learn pool shots."

"I'm willing to trade up."

She tapped her cue stick against his. "Let's see how you do with the game."

Jared leaned over the table at her urging. She explained the angles, the subtle power of the stroke, but after several tries, he was still way off the mark. She tried embracing him from behind, but had a hard time reaching around him to get into the necessary position.

"Maybe I could feel you make the shot," he suggested.

The look she sent him was skeptical, to say the least— and rightly so. But she nevertheless leaned over the table so he could tuck in behind her and lay his hands over hers on the cue. The carnal echoes of their position wasn't lost on Jared, though he tried to seem professional—or at least not as randy as he felt.

"It's all about the angles," she said softly. "And the power behind the stroke."

He swallowed around his dusty throat, thinking of something else where angles and stroking were critical.

Damn, McKenna, be a man, not a teenager.

A challenge made wildly more difficult when she shifted her stance and her backside brushed his erection. He closed his eyes, his thoughts nowhere near stick and ball sports. She smelled heavenly, a sophisticated and purely female mix of delicate flowers and warm spices. His mouth was so close to the nape of her neck he could have kissed her simply by angling his head.

She glanced at him over her shoulder. "Your stroke is too hard."

Huh? He hadn't touched her except where she'd told him to. How—

Right. Pool.

Not trusting himself to speak, he nodded.

When she faced frontward again, he prayed for control…

and patience. No woman as savvy as Victoria would fail to notice for long his lack of interest in her lesson.

With her hands beneath his, she guided the stick back, then tapped it against the glossy white cue ball, which jumped and rolled lazily to the side.

She straightened and turned, narrowing her eyes. "You're crowding me."

"I put my hands exactly where you said."

"Then you're distracting me."

He held up his palms. "Sorry."

"We'll try again."

Oh, man, do we have to?

Back in position, this time with her hands on top of his, she said, "This is an easy shot if you practice."

"Okay."

"Relax."

No possible way. "I am. You're the one who's tense."

"I'm perfectly at ease."

To prove her statement, she made the shot. Balls clanged, banked off the side of the table, then the orange five ball dropped into the corner pocket as if drawn by a magnet.

Finesse and control.

He wanted her to lose it, lose it all. "Do you get a prize?"

"Sure." She faced him. "Kicking your ass at pool is its own reward."

He held her by her waist. "Don't you want a prize?"

Her gazed tracked down his body. "Depends on what I win."

Snagging both sticks, he let them fall to the floor, and cupping her jaw, he angled her face for his kiss.

His mouth moved over hers with what he hoped was a decent amount of finesse and control. He wanted to ravage, but held the urge under tight restraint. Victoria no doubt expected and received only the best.

They fit together perfectly, and she responded to his touch without hesitancy or shyness. She caressed his tongue with her own, as committed to learning the taste and feel of him as he was with her. Jared marveled at the realization that he'd expected the weekend to be a relatively ho-hum job, but wound up with an incredibly desirable woman in his arms.

She leaned back, her gaze focused on his lips. "I thought you were pretty annoying when I first met you."

Why that truth didn't dampen his desire one bit demonstrated how quickly he'd fallen. "And now?"

She slid her hands up his chest to wrap around his neck. "You're most definitely not."

She initiated the next kiss, and he let her set the pace. Clearly, she was a woman used to taking the lead, and he wanted her to know he wasn't threatened by her doing so.

In fact, if she wanted to press him against the wall and have her carnal way with him, she could do so all night long.

When their lips parted, their breathing was choppy, their muscles tense. He was sure she wanted him as he did her. Their urges could be satisfied in a heartbeat. There were beds, chairs, floors and even pool tables all over this massive estate. He could all but feel her slim hips inviting him, her legs wrapped around him, her sighs urging him.

But uncertainty slid into her eyes as they stared at each other, and the vulnerability he saw cooled his need more than a dunk in an icy mountain river.

He captured her hand and pressed his mouth to her palm. "Let's sit on the deck."

Outside, he settled in a lounge chair, and she tucked herself between his legs, her back resting against his chest. The Atlantic spread before them, endless and mysterious. Waves crashing against the shore soothed the sharpest edge of his desire, reminding him of life's everlasting cycles.

As much as he thrived on adrenaline rushes in his job, he'd been raised on waiting. Life in Montana revolved around seasons, even years, not minutes. They waited for seeds to grow and be harvested, for cattle to breed and give birth, for winter to fade and spring to come.

Inhaling the subtle flower scent of Victoria's hair, he smiled. He could be patient. Especially since he doubted she was capable of the same.

"Can we talk about Richard's safe without spoiling the night?" she asked, looking back at him.

Richard was absolutely the last thing on Jared's mind, but she had more on her agenda than lying peacefully in the moonlight. "I guess you're gonna make his point for him."

"That's what he pays me to do." She paused, frowning. "Hopefully."

"Do you want to promote an inferior system?"

"Who says it's inferior?"

"I found flaws within twenty seconds of hearing the basic details, and what I know about security systems couldn't fill a paper cup."

"There are a variety of sophisticated safeguards with the system. Not only the ones that allow for the owner to wrongly enter the pass code, as you so astutely pointed out. Even plotters of those spy movies you're so fond of would be impressed."

"Yay for technology. But the owner of the company doesn't know those—call me crazy—vital details?"

"Richard hires the best techs. He doesn't have to be one himself."

Jared snorted.

"I suppose *your* boss knows every aspect of his business, inside and out?" she retorted.

Since he was the boss, he could answer that one with absolute honesty. "Again call him crazy, but yes."

"Why don't you like him?"

"My boss?"

"Richard."

"Do *you* like him?"

"He's my potential client," she said, her tone deadpan. "I'm wild about him."

"Fine. Terrific. But don't trust him."

"Why?"

No way Victoria would accept a vague warning. And while Jared didn't want to outright trash the guy—though he'd witnessed reasons to—he didn't want her pinning her career hopes on Richard's whims, his business sense or his honor.

Jared scooped her up and set her across his lap. Her eyes widened as she braced her hands against his shoulders. "What're you doing? We're having a serious conversation here."

"You're straining your neck to look at me, and I didn't want you to move away."

"So you're both considerate and planning to make a move on me?"

"Yes."

"Fine." She looped her arms around his neck. "Conversation first. Move later."

He wasn't known for his fast talking, but he'd figure out a way to correct that flaw. "A couple of years ago, Richard convinced me and some of my friends to invest in a project with him. He talked it up, got a lot of people involved, but when the deal went south, he conveniently got out just before it did."

"And you lost everything?"

"Not everything, but my investment. The others did, too. But good ole Rich bailed and didn't tell anyone." Jared stared out at the undulating water. "The money didn't matter so much." Remembering he wasn't supposed to have heaps of cash, he added, "Though it hurt. But I lost my trust in him. I'd worked for him and his family several times and thought we'd become friends."

"Not a friendly thing for him to do. Maybe he couldn't warn everybody in time."

Cynical, Jared shook his head. "That's what he said. Though a 'get out now' email would have done the job."

"I suppose so. How long have you known each other?"

"Not long. About three years. The only reason I told you about our history was to warn you not to rely on him."

"I don't trust anybody."

"Yeah. I get that. But ambition is seductive."

"You think I'm going to compromise myself to gain a client?"

He shrugged, sensing her temper simmering, and he had plans that included her in a happier mood. "The competition with Peter changes whatever plans you had, and since Richard's loyalties are limited to himself—and maybe his mother—you should be armed with all the information necessary to adjust your strategy."

Clearly amused by his rambling speech, she leaned close. "You're trying to protect me."

"I'm a considerate guy."

"I'm fairly self-sufficient."

"I get that." And he was starting to think he should have kept his big mouth shut, skipped the cowboy code of shielding the womenfolk, and gone straight into making his move. "Wanna kiss now?"

"Let's see." She traced her fingertip across his chest. "Do I want to discuss the underhanded way my potential client ruined a perfectly pleasant weekend by inviting my rival to participate in a competition for his lucrative contract, or would I rather have that really amazing mouth of yours fastened to mine?"

Smiling, he cupped her cheek. "We'll go slow."

True to his word, he glided his lips across hers, keeping his touch light, gentle, lingering. Though his hands tingled with the need to wander, he kept one against her cheek and the other alongside her waist. He concentrated all his effort on her mouth. He wanted every sensation focused. He wanted to tease and explore, learn her responses, inhale her sighs.

Her tongue slipped past his lips. As heat suffused his body, he held control by a fraying rope. He wanted to prolong every second, to separate himself from the rushed, demanding world where she lived.

He yearned to hold her against him, sway to an old-fashioned ballad in a dimly lit room. She'd wear a flowing dress of pale pink satin that slithered down her body with the care of a dedicated lover. He imagined candlelight flickering across her creamy skin as she smiled at him and laid her head on his shoulder. A moment suspended in time, secured by comfort.

A sudden breeze rushing off the water brought him back to reality.

They parted with her looking dazed and aroused, and him wondering how they'd gone from interest to fiery chemistry to the kind of familiarity reserved for couples who'd known each other for years.

"Should I walk you back to your room?"

She placed a kiss on his cheek. "What's your hurry?"

Her breath against his ear made his erection swell to near pain. He closed his eyes to gain control of his desire. "Absolutely none."

He was going slowly. No matter how much it killed him.

Keeping his gaze locked on hers, he slid his finger from the base of her throat over the swell of her breasts. "Can I touch you?" he asked.

Her cheeks flushed with desire. "Aren't you already?"

"Not as much as I'd like to be."

Hunger swam into her eyes. "Show me."

He pressed his lips to her pounding pulse, letting his hand drift down the center of her body, across her stomach to her thighs. Tracing the tips of his fingers over the fabric of her dress, he let them wander beyond the edge, meeting the silky skin there.

Beneath his lips, her heart beat wildly. As he moved his hand higher, heat leaped off her. He pressed his palm against the satin barrier of her panties.

Her breath caught.

He pushed aside the fabric and encountered her moist, feminine heat. His erection pulsed, and he gritted his teeth against the urge to bury his body between her legs and satisfy the aching need.

He pleasured her with his fingers, gently at first, then applying more pressure.

Her head fell back as her body arched. A low moan escaped her lips.

Watching her enjoying his technique was itself seductive. As much as he longed for the same intimate touch in return, he experienced nearly the same thrill in seeing her breathing escalate, her pupils dilate.

"Slower?" he rasped in her ear.

"Oh, my, faster." She kissed him. "Harder."

Gladly, he gave her what she wanted.

She clutched his shoulders, and he pressed his lips to the base of her throat. He loved feeling her pulse fluttering against his mouth. Victoria's encouraging response forced him to smother his own moan.

With all the day's tension, he wasn't surprised she was so quickly on the brink of release. Though he hoped he had a bit to do with the intensity of her arousal.

As his pace increased, her breathing grew choppy. When she rocked her hips against him, he increased the tempo. She gasped.

"Oh, yeah," she whispered. "Please don't stop."

No way would he. He wanted her to climax more than he wanted to take his next breath.

He wanted to swallow her moans and feel her body respond to his touch. He wanted her hips to grip his and drive them both to satisfaction.

And he absolutely had to master his own desires for any of that to happen.

When he felt her orgasm start, the hesitation, the gasp, the jerk of her hips, he buried his face against her throat, even as he kept up the pace with his fingers, absorbing every vibration.

As the shuddering subsided, she held his face and kissed

him with an enthusiasm that had his head buzzing. Plus, if he wasn't mistaken, there was a good dose of gratitude.

"That was amazing," she mumbled as her head flopped on his shoulder.

"I'm glad."

She traced his lips with her finger. "I could return the favor."

He slid his tongue over the pad, relishing the simple contact with her skin as much as he'd delighted in her rush of pleasure.

The temptation to give in to fleeting thrills was great, but he wanted more than a quick release. "I can wait," he said.

6

New York Tattletale
Lifestyles of the Wacky and Wealthy
by Peeps Galloway, Gossipmonger (And proud of it!)
As the sun peeks from behind perfect puffy white
clouds in Southampton, the well-to-do power up with
protein-laden breakfasts before their tennis dates, and
send their mistresses out the back door with a wink and
a promise of a shopping boon.

Not the way your summer is wrapping up?

Lucky for you, I'm on the gossip path and not swayed
by conventions, electrified fences, security systems or
burly bodyguards.

Speaking of security systems, the weekend party at
the Rutherford estate is sailing along, as the guests spent
last evening on a luxurious after-dinner cruise. Later,
they peeled off to their separate quarters. Or did they?

All seemed peaceful and quiet—for about fifteen
minutes. Then various lights flashed on and off all
night. An alien invasion? you might wonder.

Well…I never saw a green-tinted being or even
a character from the latest science fiction flick. But
being your dedicated and intrepid reporter, I *was* able
to clearly note not one, but *two* Balcony Encounters of

the Romantic Kind. Shadowed embraces were all the rage. Especially on Planet Earth.

(I made a recent visit to Houseman's Sporting Goods on Long Island. Bushnell has a new line of binoculars that are to die for! Mention me and receive the gossipmonger discount.)

With balmy breezes, gourmet meals and office enemies in plentiful supply, I foresee the weekend lending itself to any number of secrets revealed and liaisons consummated.

(And don't worry if nothing interesting happens, I'll just make it up or exaggerate!)

Keep your eye on the moon!

—Peeps

"So HE'S A COWBOY with discipline, smooth hands and a generous heart?"

Gathered in the kitchen with her friends, Victoria considered Calla's assessment. Over an early-morning cup of coffee, she'd told Calla and Shelby the details, including the intimate ones, about her night with Jared. "I guess so."

Calla refilled everyone's mug. "I say rope him. In fact, tie him to your bed if necessary."

Victoria frowned. "I don't rope things, much less people."

"I bet he can," Shelby interjected as she pulled a tray of orange-cranberry scones out of the oven. "Let him take control. Obviously, he knows what he's doing."

Just because she'd had the best orgasm she could remember in a while—possibly ever—was no reason to get distracted from her purpose for the weekend. She was at the estate for her career, not her libido.

Calla added more cream to her coffee. "Speaking of ropes, did you hear Katy Heinz got into the S and M crowd?"

"No kidding?" Shelby said.

Calla nodded. "Oh, yeah. She got her…well, personal parts pierced and everything."

Everyone winced and crossed their legs.

"Do you think that really makes sex better?" Calla asked into the silence.

Shelby buttered the scones. "It could add an element of the forbidden to a relationship that's gone stale."

Victoria curled her lip. "Or it could be a magnet for bacteria and various disgusting infections."

Calla rolled her eyes. "Do you have to be so pedantic?"

"Did you have to swallow your thesaurus?" Victoria retorted.

"*Pedantic* means fussy or meticulous," Calla said.

"I know what it means," she assured her. "I just don't understand why—"

"Scone?"

Victoria stared at the pastry Shelby was holding in front of her face, knowing her friend was attempting to head off an argument. "Thanks," she said as she took the pastry.

Calla selected her own scone from the tray, then stared at it moodily. "Some of us are in dire need of reviving a stale relationship."

Victoria and Shelby exchanged an awkward glance. Calla's crush on an intense NYPD detective was the source of much speculation and frustration.

"Devin will come around," Shelby said.

"Though I'm still not convinced you'll want him to," Victoria commented. "He's so temperamental. I know this great stock trader—"

"And they're not temperamental at all," Shelby said sarcastically. "Devin is loyal as well as gorgeous. That's always a good place to start."

"He's also protective," Calla said. When her friends looked skeptical, she added, "He's a cop."

Victoria swallowed a mouthful of scone, which, like everything Shelby made, was delicious. "Seems to me he'd be better at the shooting aspects of his job, rather than the protecting and serving parts."

Calla planted her hand on her hip. "And your cowboy would be better off with a woman whose boots were made from rattlesnake skin in Austin instead of being hand-stitched by Italian nuns in Florence."

Victoria scowled. "He's not my cowboy."

Calla appeared thrilled. "Oh, so you won't mind if I go after him?"

Victoria narrowed her eyes. "Try it and die."

Her friend leaned her forearms against the tiled island in the center of the kitchen. "Since you're so into this guy, are you actually gonna do all the water sports instead of sitting by the pool with a low-fat smoothie and a big hat?"

"Why would I change my plans for a guy?" Victoria asked, certain the answer would be obvious as well as rhetorical.

"'Cause he's *not* a stocktrader and he's smokin' hot," Calla said, as if *this* was the obvious response.

She certainly couldn't dispute Jared's hotness, but didn't see any reason to ignore her corner office ambition because of it.

"He's also charming and considerate," Shelby said. "And with water sports you get to see him with very few clothes on."

"Oh, man." Calla's eyelashes fluttered closed, graphically proving the point. "He's got a great chest."

Shelby put down her scone to point. "Plus, there's the great orgasm."

"No telling how many more you could get in before the weekend's out," Calla commented.

Shelby nodded in agreement. "She'd be less cranky."

Calla smiled. "Which might actually lead to her getting the contract."

"Peter would appreciate her restored confidence due to physical satisfaction," Shelby said.

Despite her annoyance at yet again being discussed as if she wasn't present, Victoria asked, "Why would Peter care?"

As Shelby arranged the remaining scones onto a platter,

she said, "Because you're liable to smother him with a pillow in his sleep to get the contract otherwise."

Victoria knew her goals weren't easily obtainable, but she wasn't irrational. Or homicidal. "You're suggesting I'd resort to murder to win this contract?"

Her friends stared at her. "Wouldn't surprise me," Shelby muttered.

"Me, either," Calla added, quickly sipping coffee.

Victoria didn't enjoy being the butt of jokes, especially since she was the one of their band of three who was known to make the biting, sarcastic comments. What was happening to her? A few hours in the moonlight as the object of Jared's benevolent touch, and she was losing her edge. "Are either of you actually going to offer any remotely reasonable advice on how I can enjoy Jared and keep my focus on winning this contract at the same time?"

Shelby cracked eggs and whipped them with cream in a bowl. "Contract during the day, Jared at night."

After twenty minutes, that's what they'd come up with? She could've slept later. "Really? That's all you've got?"

"Sounds reasonable to me," Calla said.

"That's too simple to work," Victoria insisted.

Calla nudged Shelby. "In addition to being pedantic, she also has a bizarre tendency toward the complex." Calla grinned at Victoria. "Care to comment, Vicky?"

Keeping her tone only mildly threatening, even though she *was* now feeling homicidal, she wiped a dribble of coffee from the side of her mug. "I'm hovering between carnal satisfaction and career destruction. You really want to push me with the Vicky business?"

Her friends each slung an arm around her shoulder. "This weekend won't break your career," Shelby said.

Calla nodded. "Work might be better if you get the contract, but it's not like Coleman PR is gonna suddenly banish you to the mail room."

Oh, sure. They'd never do that to The Legend's daughter.

She already had a successful career. She was respected and well paid. What more could anyone want?

And yet the pressure to go further, rise higher never seemed to ease. No matter what she accomplished, she couldn't find the peak. If Peter beat her, she'd be beyond humiliated. She couldn't watch her colleagues either gloat or struggle to commiserate.

So, yeah, career destruction was the best description she could come up with.

Maybe Calla would loan her a thesaurus, and she could find another metaphor, which she could use to explain to her mother why she was the weak link in the Holmes genetic line of success.

Mrs. Keegan, who'd been setting out dishes for the breakfast buffet in the dining room, bustled into the kitchen. "The Standishes are wanting breakfast."

Shelby glanced at the clock. "The mini quiches need two more minutes. But go ahead and take the chafing dishes of French toast and bacon. I'll follow you with the scones."

Calla set aside her mug. "We'll help."

The four women toted dishes and trays to the buffet server in the dining room, and when they returned to the kitchen, they found Jared pouring himself a cup of coffee.

"Ladies." His gaze locked on Victoria's. "Sleep well?"

Until I woke up sweaty and horny at 4:00 a.m., you bet, Victoria thought.

Calla poked her in the back. "Um, yeah," Victoria said. "You?"

"Not bad." He sipped his coffee. "Ready for some fun on the Jet Ski today?"

Oh, my... Involuntarily, Victoria licked her lips. How was it possible for a man to look so perfect wearing merely a T-shirt and jeans? "Sure, I—"

"Actually," Calla interrupted, "V was planning to sit by the pool awhile. Maybe later."

Victoria glared at her friend, whose expression turned

smug. No doubt she was remembering the I-don't-change-plans-for-a-man discussion.

"But let's all go," Calla suggested brightly, forcing Victoria to grind her teeth. "Right after breakfast. I could use a bracing swim."

"You said you were going to take pictures," Shelby reminded her.

Calla's smile was gleeful. "I was, but I've impulsively *changed my plans.*"

"Oh, good grief," Victoria grumbled.

"Have a scone," Shelby said, offering one to Jared.

No doubt the move was an effort to head off Victoria's impulse to clobber Calla.

Looking as though he'd rather be anywhere other than where he was, Jared bit into his scone.

Way to be seductive, Victoria.

Shelby grabbed Calla's arm and pulled her from the room. "Let's go check on the buffet."

"But—"

Ignoring the protest, she closed the door behind them.

Proving his easy manner and patience were infinite, Jared propped himself against the counter next to Victoria. "*V,* huh? Not a very imaginative nickname."

"It's the only one I answer to."

Leaning close, he dragged his index finger up the center of her body. "Surely I can do better."

As seemed to be the norm with him, she found her head buzzing and her extremities tingling. The memories of his touch, his kiss, were fresh in her mind, intensifying her need. She should be planning what to say to Richard over breakfast, or trying to intimidate Peter into bailing from the weekend.

"Vicky's out," Jared whispered against her ear.

Considerate.

He was hot, smart, fun, generous and considerate. No matter how the competition for the contract went, she had no hope of resisting him.

"What about Tori?" he asked, brushing his lips across her cheek.

Victoria tried to concentrate. "With a *y* or an *i?*"

"Does it matter?"

"One's a stripper's name, one's a conservative English political party."

"I should have known. Tia?"

"Again, stripper."

"Vic?"

"Is there a reason you can't call me by my whole name?"

"It's long." He placed a lingering kiss beneath her jaw. "In the heat of passion, I need something to gasp."

Victoria had to swallow her own gasp. The man was forever saying something outrageous. Something tempting.

Smiling, she laid her hand on his cheek. His brown eyes were warm with need and completely focused on her. "Maybe—"

That's when they heard a bloodcurdling scream coming from upstairs.

JARED WAS THE FIRST TO REACH Rose's bedroom, where the terrified sound had come from.

Given her tendency toward drama, he wasn't too concerned. Maybe her nail polish had clotted? Still, he pulled her into his arms when he saw her shaking in a corner. "It's okay. You're safe."

"Oh, Jared," she sobbed against his chest. "I'm so glad you're here. It's horrible."

He patted her back as he heard several other people rush into the room. "Don't worry."

"What happened?" Victoria asked calmly.

Behind her stood the rest of the household, most looking shocked, some suspicious. Rose's tendency toward drama was well-known.

"My necklace," she wailed. "It's gone!"

Again, Victoria was the first to speak. "You mean the necklace you wore last night?"

"Yes." Rose covered her face with one hand and clung tighter to Jared. "My beautiful necklace. It's been stolen."

Parting the crowd, Richard strode into the room, obviously intending to take charge. "What's happened?"

Jared wondered if he'd practiced his authoritative expression in the mirror.

"My necklace!" Rose wailed again.

With his shirt only partially buttoned, Sal shoved his way into the room and rushed to Rose's side, pulling her into his arms as Jared stepped away. "There, there. Don't cry. You've simply misplaced your necklace. What did you do with it after you took it off?"

She pointed a trembling finger to her antique wardrobe. "I put it in the safe."

Richard moved in that direction. "I'm sure it's here."

"It's not! It's gone!"

While Richard examined the small safe on the wardrobe floor, Jared's gaze moved to Victoria. She looked as speculative as everybody else, and he shrugged.

After her accusation that he and Rose had once been lovers, her throwing herself in his arms had an entirely different meaning for the two of them.

He liked the private conversation going on, even though not a word was exchanged. He'd always put a fair amount of stock into body language, but with Victoria, the implications took on greater meaning. She was a demanding woman with a gentle side, and after last night, he was all the more curious about how much more lay beneath the surface.

She had him hooked like a fish on a line. Except he had no intention of escaping.

Richard's face was white as he turned. "It's not here."

Rose looked pleadingly at Jared, as if he could save her. "I told you."

"Don't worry, Rose," he said. "We'll find it."

"Of course we will." Her smile bright, Calla rushed forward from the crowd gathered in the doorway. "We'll retrace your steps from last night. I'm sure—"

Richard stormed past Calla to his mother's side, grabbing her upper arm. "Was the safe open or closed when you got up this morning?"

"It was open." Angry tears filled her eyes as she wrenched away from her son and moved closer to Sal. "That's why I walked over there and looked inside."

"You're sure it was open?" Richard pressed.

Rose's temper was beginning to take over from shock. *"Yes."*

Richard paced beside her. "You couldn't have locked it in the safe, Mother."

Was he trying to convince himself, her or everyone else?

Most likely all three.

For if the necklace was missing, and Rose *had* locked it in the safe, then somebody in the house was a thief, and Richard's precious new invention had failed.

Which would be lovely justice if it wasn't so disturbing. And damned inconvenient.

How was Jared supposed to enjoy, and ultimately seduce, Victoria if Rose was crying, Richard was pacing and the rest of them were wondering who had a valuable necklace stuffed in his or her luggage?

"We need to call the police," Victoria said firmly when everyone else seemed shocked into silence.

"Yes." Relief washed over Rose's mottled face. "The police will sort all this out."

Mrs. Keegan nodded. "I'll take care of it, Mrs. Rutherford."

Before anybody could move, Richard slashed out with his hand. *"No."*

Ruthie rushed to her husband's side. "Darling, this isn't something we should handle alone."

Victoria joined the group around Rose. "Ruthanne's right. There's obviously been a break-in. The police need to come and examine the scene, get statements from all of us. We should go downstairs and wait for them, so we don't contaminate the evidence any more than we already have."

"We're not calling the police," Richard insisted.

Jared raised his eyebrows. "If a crime's been committed, I'm pretty sure we don't have a choice."

Richard's smile was smug. "This is Southampton. We do what we like."

Could the guy sound any more like an arrogant weasel?

Ruthanne squeezed her husband's arm. "Shouldn't we leave this kind of thing to the experts?"

"And open the company to negative publicity?" he asked incredulously. "Absolutely not. Besides, we have an expert. Victoria is here."

"Sure I am," she said calmly, then paused and shook her head. *"What?"*

"You can deal with the missing necklace," he said, his voice firm.

She looked as confused as everybody else. "How? What do I know about police procedure?"

Jared was also wondering how this was in any way Victoria's problem.

"Your father's a lawyer," Richard stated.

She shook her head. "He's a corporate attorney, not a criminal one."

"You just said the scene needs to be examined, and we should get statements." Richard's tone was stubborn. "You know about contaminated evidence."

Astonishment flickered across Victoria's face, followed quickly by a sarcastic tone in her voice. "Of course I do. I read crime novels on vacation."

"But, V, last spring we did—"

Victoria stepped in front of Calla. "We did. That's right, we went to the movies and saw that new courtroom drama. I must admit I did figure out who the bad guy was pretty early on."

Seeing Victoria's bold, fake smile, Jared stifled a chuckle.

He'd love to know what she and her friend had actually done. "I agree with Victoria," he said, moving toward the bedroom doorway, where Shelby, David and the Standishes hovered. "Let's go downstairs and talk this out. Rose could use some tea and breakfast."

"This is my house, McKenna," Richard said as he marched from the room. "I'm in charge here."

Jared exchanged a frustrated look with Victoria. Richard in command?

Heaven help them all.

7

SITTING ON THE SOFA WITH CALLA and David, Victoria sipped coffee from an elegant Dresden china cup Mrs. Keegan had set out for the guests.

The housekeeper darted about the room while the people she served twitched, glanced around and whispered to one another.

Had there been a break-in?

If so, the porcelain Victoria held in her hand was probably as valuable as anything. Why wasn't it taken?

Moreover there were paintings, electronic equipment, sets of silver, as well as other pieces of jewelry still sitting around Rose's bedroom. Victoria had seen both a genuine pearl necklace and diamond tennis bracelet on the dresser. If a professional thief had sneaked in, why not scoop up the lot? No extra time or effort required.

No, a break-in didn't make sense. Which meant one of the people in the parlor was a thief.

Richard was in both denial and CYA mode, and Victoria knew she was caught in the middle. She had to placate her client and somehow not break the law. Question was, how could she use this development to her advantage in winning the PR campaign?

Maybe the very idea was coldblooded. Maybe she should

include herself in the group of women surrounding Rose, holding her hand and assuring her everything would be fine. Maybe, like Peter, she should be talking in quiet tones with Richard, assuring him he was a wise leader and handling the unexpected situation with brilliance. Maybe she should join Calla and David's ludicrous conversation about them all being trapped by a vicious storm, then murdered off one by one by an ax-wielding psycho from the village.

David, who'd suggested the theory, obviously didn't realize he'd been tossed into the midst of Robin Hood's gang, not an Agatha Christie movie.

Victoria refused to submit to the last, desperate thought that flashed through her mind. *Call Mother. She'll know what to do.*

No. She drank more coffee, the hot liquid soothing her urge to panic. Her mother would have had the contract signed five minutes after she walked in the manor door. *That's what legends do.*

Jared knelt beside the sofa. "I bet ole Rich is regretting not giving his mother the retina scan model of his super wonderful safe now."

Grateful to set the image of her own mother aside, Victoria choked back a laugh. In fact, this whole situation was ironically hilarious. Or would be, if she wasn't the one getting screwed by it.

"If you find the necklace, do you get the contract?" he asked quietly.

The fact that he'd guessed the direction of her thoughts spoke to his sensitivity and their unique connection.

Since there was no way she was that transparent.

"I guess so." She dragged her gaze from Rose in Vulnerability mode to look at Jared. Much better view. "This puts a damper on your wild adventure weekend."

He crossed his arms over his broad chest. "I get paid regardless. But I'd rather be out there than in here. Are you going to press the issue of calling the cops?"

"I don't think so. Rose could've misplaced the necklace. Shouldn't we look for it first?"

"And compromise the crime scene?"

She swallowed, caught by her own logic. And ethics. "I said that impulsively."

"Because you're right. Calling the police is the right thing to do."

"Who says?"

His eyes flashed with annoyance. "Anybody with integrity."

"I'm sure they have insurance."

"So you don't care if a thief gets away?"

"Absolutely, I care. But I don't see how I can change anything."

"You want the contract more." He sighed as a look of disappointment moved across his handsome face. Leaning close, he rasped, "I warned you about Richard's lack of ethics. Be sure you don't follow him down that road."

As Jared walked away, Victoria scowled at his back. That high-handed, self-righteous...

Before she could come up with another, more scathing adjective, Richard appeared in front of her. "I need your help," he said.

Since she was either going to get a crick in her neck staring up at him or Calla and David were going to add a new layer to their already crazy plot, she rose. When she and Richard found a bit more privacy in the corner of the room, she admitted, "I don't know anything about solving crimes."

"Sure you do. Ruthanne read about you and your friends catching a big-time swindler this past spring."

Damn that Peeps Galloway. "Pure gossip," Victoria said, tossing her hair back. "You know how they love to make something out of nothing."

"Exactly. If the police come to investigate, the media will hear about it, and they'll print all kinds of lies about how my safe failed, how I can't protect my own family, and why should the public trust me? It's a PR nightmare."

But his safe *had* failed, he hadn't protected his own family and maybe the public *shouldn't* trust his products.

"How did this happen, anyway?" she asked, knowing she couldn't reveal her thoughts. "Did the safe look like it had been broken into?"

"No scratch marks or a crowbar lying around, if that's what you mean. Besides, you can't force the door open that way. It would trigger the alarm."

Yeah, sure. A gnat landing on the handle would supposedly set off the alarm, and yet some Houdini had managed to pull off the impossible. "Is there a way to check when the code was entered?" She left off the implied *maybe it was an inside job.*

Richard's face flushed. "Not really."

A migraine started in her temples. "What about spy-quality fail-safes? What happened to James Bond not being able to crack the technology?"

"We haven't gotten all the bugs worked out on those features yet."

Terrific.

But when had Victoria let a little thing like absolute truth get in the way of a successful campaign? Some things were hidden for the greater good.

If she could save Richard from the nightmare, or better yet, prevent the gloom from descending at all, she'd definitely get the contract. Renowned, maybe not. But it would be a start.

Whenever her mother was introduced at a conference, meeting or even cocktail party, it was *"the legendary Joanne Holmes."* A revered hush filled the room when her father, the lawyer, entered. So the thought of no longer being the daughter who couldn't live up to her parents' brilliance was enticing beyond measure.

Richard clutched her hand. "You have to help me, Victoria."

She squeezed back. "Certainly I will."

"We'll probably find it in a laundry hamper or something."

"Maybe." Could she be that lucky? "But if we can't, and we eventually have to call the police, how are we going to get around the fact that we didn't phone them when the theft actually happened?"

"We'll tell them we only just noticed the necklace was missing."

Victoria hid her wince. Now Richard had them all lying to the police. Not to mention there were twelve individuals who knew the truth. A conspiracy among that many people would last about twelve minutes.

She'd have to make Richard sign the contract before they got arrested.

Her gaze slid to the group around Rose, which now included Calla. Calla who was friends—and possibly more—with an NYPD detective. A detective who'd recently caught her and her friends breaking into a downtown Manhattan office building and had looked the other way in order to get the evidence needed to uncover a big-time swindler.

If they did have to call the police, at least she knew somebody who might be both discreet and not too picky about the timing of the report.

Not that the NYPD had any jurisdiction over Southampton.

She'd been handed this disaster for five minutes and already she could see twenty potential complications. "Get everybody to go outside with Jared. Let them continue with the original water sports plan. Mrs. Keegan and I will stay in the house and do a full search."

"Including everybody's luggage?"

No way Victoria could hide her wince now. "Let's tackle one thing at a time. If the necklace has been misplaced, we won't need to go there. Mrs. Keegan and I will look in the rooms together, but not pick through personal possessions, yet."

"And if you don't come up with anything?"

Was she actually going to interrogate her friends and colleagues? Rummage through their unmentionables? Even Sal and David's? And Richard's mother's, his wife's? And even the man himself?

Could it really be an inside job? What if this was some kind of insurance scam?

No, that didn't make sense. At least not a scam perpetrated by Richard. He'd never have gotten his own safe involved, and he'd be calling the police himself, so he could get the theft documented quickly.

"Then we start retracing everybody's steps from last night," she said, echoing Calla's earlier suggestion. "We find out who was unaccounted for and when."

"You really think it was one of us?"

"Do you think the house and the safe's security were both compromised?"

Richard's face paled. "Good point." He brushed his lips across her cheek. "Brilliant as always. I'll leave this to you."

He immediately laid out his plans to go ahead with the day, assuring everyone the necklace had most likely been misplaced and would no doubt turn up by the afternoon.

Within minutes, the nervous guests had changed into bathing suits and were heading out the kitchen door toward the dock.

Jared spared Victoria no more than a passing glance as he walked beside Emily Standish, promising her she'd be a natural on skis.

Victoria assumed a stiff wind would blow tiny Emily off the boat before she ever dived in the water. But she would be enjoying the sight of Jared's bare chest all day, so Emily was sure to have more fun than Victoria, regardless of how the wind blew.

She was aware that she was choosing Richard over Jared, and that Jared would certainly see things that way. The loss disturbed her more than she'd expected. But the cowboy adventurer, desirable as he might be, was a weekend fling at best. Richard was the key to her dreams coming true.

"I'm going to need your help to perform a search of the house," Victoria said in a quiet voice to the housekeeper as they stood next to the kitchen island.

Mrs. Keegan, who'd apparently seen stranger things going on in the Rutherford household, appeared unsurprised at being drafted into service. "Let me finish tidying the dining room, and I'll be right with you."

Shelby closed the door behind the group of guests, then turned to face Victoria, her expression incredulous. "He's not calling the police?"

"No."

"And you think this is going to get you the PR contract?"

"Yes."

"How are you going to move into your fancy new corner office from jail?"

"I'm not going to jail."

"What about me, Calla, your gorgeous cowboy? Don't you think we'd rather hang on to our freedom? You're willing to risk us all?"

"Nobody's going to jail."

"Uh-huh." Shelby went toward the pantry, returning with bags of sugar and flour. "So you're paying for my attorney when the cops aren't quite so easygoing?"

"I seem to recall risking my neck recently for a certain friend." Victoria tapped her finger against her lips. "Who was that, I wonder?"

"That was entirely different. My parents were on the brink of bankruptcy, and we did report the crime to the police. Plus, we were trying to catch a criminal, not commit crimes ourselves."

"Oh? Maybe you don't recall the break-in at a certain downtown office building?"

Shelby's face turned as red as her hair. "That was different. I was—"

"Fighting for truth, justice and the American way. I remember the speech."

"You won't get everybody to agree to this."

"Oh, please. I already have. You and Calla are loyal to me, and everybody else will do what Richard says."

"Including Jared and Mrs. Keegan?"

"Naturally. They work for the Rutherfords. They won't risk their jobs."

"What about Sal and David?"

Victoria waved her hand. "Sal's crazy about Rose. David works for him. All one happy—"

"Dysfunctional," Shelby interjected.

"—family," Victoria finished.

"What about the Standishes?" Shelby asked peevishly. "Maybe Peter's not willing to go to jail for a contract."

"Nobody's going to jail," Victoria repeated, her tone firm. After all, she needed to convince herself as well as her friend. "We don't even know a crime's been committed. Rose probably stuck it in a drawer by accident."

"I can't imagine anybody forgetting where they put a necklace that elaborate and valuable. She seemed pretty certain she'd locked it away." Shelby's gaze met Victoria's. "In that state-of-the-art, foolproof safe you're going to try to convince people to buy."

"Which no one will purchase if they think it doesn't work."

"If it doesn't work, Richard shouldn't be selling it."

Embarrassed by Shelby's honesty, Victoria sagged against the counter. "Okay, so there are a few…bugs to work out. Richard admitted so. But he won't have a chance to work on them if his product's reputation is ruined before it ever gets launched."

Shelby dumped measured ingredients in a bowl. "Rationalizing the moral compromise. I've been there."

"The spirit of the law," Victoria argued back.

"How does not reporting a crime fall anywhere within the law?"

"When losing this contract might cause an even bigger crime to occur."

"Bigger how?"

"I'm going to strangle Peter Standish with my bare hands if he tells Richard how brilliant he is one more time."

Shelby pulled a lump of dough from the bowl and kneaded. "I see your point."

But was her success worth this pact she'd made with Richard? Was Victoria crossing some ethical line she could never retreat from? Had she already flown to the other side, and wasn't even aware of booking a ticket?

"Am I crazy, Shel?" she murmured.

"A bit. But aren't we all when it comes to getting what we want?"

"You were a little nuts about Trevor, as I recall."

Shelby's smile held a world of pleasurable memories. "Not was. Still am."

I should want that.

Victoria blinked as the idea slid into her mind. Why hadn't she ever wanted a man to share secrets with? The same man, day after day, night after night. A man she was devoted to, instead of a job or a contract or an office.

Yet the cold formality of her parents always held her back. She'd rather be alone than have that kind of relationship. So she deliberately dated "rich jocks" as Calla liked to call them. That realization was sobering, as well.

"I bet Sal Columbo had something to do with the theft," Shelby said, breaking into Victoria's thoughts. "His eyes were shifty. He could be an international jewel thief, dating Rose to get his hands on that necklace. He was the one who brought up the story about it, if you remember."

Victoria cocked her head. "Did you have a spy novel for breakfast? I think he's perfectly nice. And we haven't determined anything's been stolen yet."

"Right." Shelby's tone dripped with sarcasm. "That multimillion-dollar necklace is in the laundry hamper."

THE NECKLACE WASN'T IN THE hamper or any other place Rose could have accidentally dropped it.

Victoria and Mrs. Keegan searched every inch of the woman's bedroom, plus retraced her steps around the house from dinner to bedtime. They both recalled that Rose hadn't been wearing the necklace during the boat ride, so there was no worry that it had been lost at sea or outside the house.

Had she locked the necklace in the safe right after dinner, or had she waited until before turning in for the night?

That was the first question to ask when Victoria spoke to her.

And was she really going to question everyone? How was she qualified for interrogation?

Harvard Business School had never prepared her for days like this.

"I didn't take it!" Mrs. Keegan exclaimed.

Victoria focused on the distraught housekeeper. "I never said you did."

Her eyes filled with tears. "But everybody's thinking so. I thought Mrs. Rutherford trusted me." She sniffled. "Both of them."

"I'm sure they trust you." Awkwardly, Victoria patted the other woman's shoulder. She was useless around crying women. "Let's go downstairs and see if Shelby needs any help with lunch."

Her friend would know how to comfort the housekeeper.

"Any luck?" Shelby asked as soon as they walked into the kitchen.

Victoria shook her head.

True to her prediction, Shelby noticed the housekeeper's tears and rushed over to pull her into a hug. Patting the older woman's back, she assured her that no one with any sense would think she was guilty of the theft.

Keeping her opinion to herself, Victoria decided that the only people she was taking off the suspect list were herself, Shelby and Calla. Everybody else was subject to scrutiny.

After sending Mrs. Keegan to her room to splash some water on her face and repair her makeup, Shelby poured Victoria a glass of lemonade.

"Do you suspect Jared?"

Anybody with integrity. Jared's words from earlier reverberated through her head, making any accusation against him seem silly. "I should," she said, frustrated by the idea that she was probably thinking with her libido and not her head. "I know less about him than anybody."

"Except Sal Columbo."

"And the designer-suited assistant, David Greggory. He looks more like a potential jewel thief."

"You can't be serious about David. His shoes are too shiny."

Sometimes her buddy's logic—or lack thereof—was totally lost on her. "Too shiny?"

"Trevor has the same ones, and they require an exacting touch to polish. Seriously, the man can spend hours at it."

First, Victoria would have thought a guy with Trevor's sizable bank account would have had some lackey polish his shoes. And second…well, second really rolled right into third, fourth and fifth reasons that she could name why footwear couldn't possibly have anything to do with one's tendency toward thievery. "Seems to me an exacting touch is exactly what was used to get into the safe."

"Fair point."

Victoria sipped her lemonade. "You honestly think that sweet old man is a thief?"

"Who knows what anybody's capable of, given the right motivation?"

No argument there. "Did Sal spend the night in Rose's bedroom?"

"No idea. But I suspect there's going to be a very uncomfortable conversation with the lady of the house later."

Victoria tried not to wince. Even if she did find the necklace, she was dearly afraid that, in the process, she'd find out more about the Rutherford family than she ever wished to know.

"So we eliminate nobody at this point?" her friend asked.

"Us." Victoria paused. "And Jared."

Shelby nodded in agreement before heading to the pantry, then returning with tomatoes. "How are you going to find out who did it?"

She had a couple of ideas, and there was no reason she couldn't put them to the test while wearing her new bikini and ogling the strong and sexy Jared. Thanks to a dedication to Pilates and spin class, she looked pretty good in a bathing suit, so—

Hang on. She pinned Shelby in place with her glare. "How am *I* going to find out? What about one for all and all for one?"

"That's the Three Musketeers, not Robin Hood, but the gang's all here, so I guess *we're* going to find out."

"We're not a gang," Victoria reminded her.

"Yeah, yeah." Shelby positioned a tomato on the cutting board and began slicing. "I'm breaking the law—again, I might add—for a loved one."

"Who says we're breaking the law?"

"Isn't there something about aiding and abetting?"

Victoria shook her head. "That only applies if you drive the getaway car for a bank robber."

"You're assuming." Shelby dumped the tomatoes in a bowl, then headed to the fridge. "We should call Detective Antonio. We need advice."

"He's more likely to arrest us."

"Nah. He has a thing for Calla."

Though Victoria had seen the cop's avid interest first-hand, he never seemed to do anything about it, even when Calla flirted with him. Something was seriously wrong with that guy.

Sure, V, judge everybody else. You're currently selling your conscience for a promotion.

"We're not calling the cops," Victoria said firmly. "We're going to—"

"Damn, damn, damn." Shelby, standing at the open freezer, slammed her hand against the stainless-steel handle.

Victoria rushed to her side. "What? You found the necklace?"

"No. When I was getting out the herbs for the gazpacho, I noticed my veal was missing. Somebody's put it in the freezer. Hell, even if it defrosts in time, I can't serve lamb that's been frozen."

Personally, Victoria ate frozen, then microwaved dinners all the time at her desk, but felt got a measure of Shelby's panic. This was an important weekend for her catering business's reputation. Only the best would do.

"I'll have to go into the village." Shelby wiped her hands on her chef's apron. "Maybe Mrs. K can finish making lunch."

Victoria caught her arm. "I'll go into the village. You keep working on lunch."

"What about the interrogation?"

"I'd rather save it for lunchtime. I can hardly ask personal questions while I'm hanging on for dear life on the back of a Jet Ski."

"If you're sure…"

The back door swung open and David stumbled into the kitchen. "Save me, please." Wide-eyed and seeming exhausted, the venerable assistant collapsed into a chair at the table. "That man is crazy."

"Jared?" Victoria ventured.

David nodded. "I don't really like water, loud engines or anything that moves fast. I had a bad experience at summer camp as a kid. But he convinced me to go out with him on the Jet Ski by telling me it was more secure than regular skis."

"Surely you went slowly," Shelby said, handing him a glass of lemonade.

Nodding in thanks, he gulped the drink. "Not slowly enough. I threw up as we rolled over the first wave."

Shelby cringed. "Oh, dear."

Victoria took pity on him, given his flushed face and agitated expression, but could also hear her mother whispering advice. *Vulnerable people are agreeable.* Then Jared. *Anybody with integrity... Be sure you don't follow him down that road.*

She'd agreed to help Richard. She needed that promotion.

Interrogation, or Jared in a swimsuit? Victoria struggled longer than she would have a few days ago.

Hell.

As always, her career won.

"How about a trip into the village?" she suggested to David, with what she hoped was a comforting smile.

DRIVING INTO TOWN WITH DAVID in the passenger's seat, Victoria knew what she had to do, and was surprised by the guilt she couldn't shake. "You said you went to camp as a kid. Where'd you grow up?"

He ran his hand over the Mercedes's black leather seat with a touch bordering on loving. "Brooklyn."

"No kidding?" Victoria glanced at him. "I'm a city kid, too."

"Manhattan, I'll bet."

"Yeah." After another glimpse at his stony face, she added, "My parents are well-off."

"Mine weren't. My mom worked hard, but never really got anywhere much. 'Course, I don't know about my dad." His breathing hitched.

Terrific. Some interrogator she was. She'd been at it five minutes and had already asked a question that upset her interrogee. Maybe this was harder than it looked on TV. "No kidding?" she said neutrally, hoping to prod him to give more information.

Ambition really had no shame.

"He left when I was three," David continued. "I guess I didn't measure up. Of course I—" He stopped, his hand moving to the window button. "I need air."

"Sure you do." Remorse washed over her. "Breathe deep. You'll be fine."

David wheezed.

She'd honestly considered him a suspect. But he had even more family issues than she did, plus he didn't have much in the way of chutzpah. If anything, this theft required guts.

She let him recover as she drove along the coast and into the village of Southampton. Quaint shops and cozy boutiques lined the streets, and Victoria knew from experience that the service within was exemplary and the selection of products both high quality and expensive.

She found the butcher with ease, thanks to Mrs. K's precise directions, and the veal was wrapped and ready. On her way out of the shop, she spotted a familiar name, printed in scripted letters on a building across the street.

"Colombo Jewelers," she murmured. "Sal's?" she asked David, who leaned against the car, dabbing his face with a handkerchief.

"Yes, though his sons run the business now. He also has a few branches in the city. Would you like a tour?"

Glad to see his coloring was stronger, and intrigued by the connection between Rose's friend and precious gems, Victoria nodded. "Definitely."

Wilting in the heat, David readily agreed. He seemed more at ease as he approached the door with the gilded handle.

Embraced by air-conditioning, Victoria smiled politely at the uniformed guard who opened the door. *If Rose had one of those, she wouldn't be in this situation....*

David led her toward the center of the shop, where a saleswoman greeted him with familiarity, while Victoria cast her gaze down into the cases. Sparkling gems glinted back at her with seductive invitation.

How easy would it be to whip out a credit card and have glamour decorate her skin?

How many women had lost their senses to such false perfection?

Surrounded by luxury but not much affection, Victoria didn't appreciate the appeal of jewels much anymore. When she was younger, she'd delighted in having a touch of glitter on her arms and fingers. But as she grew older, she understood how hard someone had to work to acquire luxuries, and she found herself more and more seduced by time, not flash.

She liked spending the hours she didn't work with her friends. She liked giving to those who struggled. She liked long plane flights so she could indulge in a good novel without the constant interruption of her cell phone. She liked seeing the appreciation in a man's eyes when she took extra time to dress, and find just the right enticing scent.

Okay, that was a new one.

Jared's influence, no doubt.

Was the acquisition of more and more things really why she worked so hard? When she moved into her senior VP office and redecorated, would she be satisfied? When her parents finally acknowledged her accomplishments, would she be happy?

"See anything you like?" the saleswoman asked.

Staring down at the jewel-ladened case in earnest, and not expecting to find anything to tempt her, she spotted a ring studded with twined sapphires and diamonds the color of chocolate. The colors were a melding of her and Jared's eyes. "That one."

After slipping the ring on Victoria's middle finger, the saleswoman went on about the origin of the gems, their quality and value.

Victoria hardly listened. She blew out an excited breath

and saw the joining of her and Jared's bodies. The idea was silly, the purchase frivolous. The weekend was about her professional future. Her promotion was on the line. Her family's respect of her hung in the balance.

Job and interrogation forgotten, she handed over her credit card. She walked out of the shop with the ring on her finger and a gleeful smile on her face as she drove back to the Rutherford estate.

David congratulated her on her shrewd purchase. Chocolate-colored diamonds were all the rage.

Victoria curled her hand into a fist as they approached the back door leading to the kitchen. She only wanted to see Jared. Crazy maybe. But that just continued the mania that had enveloped her and her friends lately.

Righting wrongs. Stealing from the rich to give to the poor.

And though she was rich in jewels, she was poor in truth. Poor in sincerity.

But after this promotion, after she proved to her parents she was worthy of the Holmes name, she was going to change things.

When David excused himself to go to his room, and Mrs. K had taken the veal off to marinate, Shelby grabbed Victoria's arm. "Did you learn anything about who he is? Where he's from?"

"I did," Victoria replied. "But I don't think he's our guy. Too normal."

"If you say so." Shelby pulled a tray of cold cuts from the fridge. "Listen, the sooner we figure out where everybody was and when, the closer we'll be to finding the thief."

"Bringing us back to the uncomfortable conversation with Rose about whether or not she slept alone last night. Not a task I'm looking forward to."

Victoria definitely needed to get her alone for that little chat. Or should she…? Rose liked Jared. Maybe Victoria could get him to soften her up first. And since he wasn't so thrilled with her taking on this matter, and didn't seem to be inclined to be her assistant investigator, maybe she could soften Jared with her new bikini.

Okay, maybe not soften, exactly.

"I'm guessing this is for lunch," she said to Shelby.

"Gazpacho. Fruit. And sandwiches on homemade bread."

"Why don't you set everything out by the pool? I'll get changed, then go down and call everyone over."

Shelby's expression was suspicious. "And that relates to interrogation how?"

"I think you'll see the connection."

8

PULLING ON A T-SHIRT AS HE stepped off the boat, Jared nearly stumbled when he spotted Victoria standing on the dock wearing a bright yellow bikini.

"Damn her," he muttered.

Tall, lean and stunning, she spoke briefly to the guests who passed her, but her focus was on him.

He wanted her and wished he didn't. He craved her touch and knew he'd be satisfied only when he got it. He understood where her loyalties lay and longed to change them.

When he was mere steps away from her, he watched Richard clutch her hand as she shook her head. Richard nodded, a stiff jerk, then headed to the house.

So the task he'd pushed on her hadn't gone well.

Not surprising.

"Hi," she said as Jared attempted to walk past her. "How's the water?"

"Refreshing. How's the search for the necklace?"

"Bad." Her eyes danced with promise as she trailed her finger down his chest. "Is there anything you don't know about?"

She was going to seduce him into going along with Richard's secret? Crap, Jared had expected more. Or at least better. "There's plenty, but I know when I'm being played."

When he turned to leave, she grabbed his hand. "I'm not playing you."

He leaned in. "I'm not Richard Rutherford's lapdog."

She let go and stepped back. "Neither am I."

"Coulda fooled me."

"I need this contract."

"And you think I need you enough to help you get it."

"Do you?"

He let his gaze drift down her body. "You're offering a trade?"

She stared at the distant horizon. "I could use your help."

"You don't want to grill me about my alibi, search my luggage?"

"No. I was with you till nearly two. Though I don't even know when the necklace was taken." She sighed. "I've got to talk to Rose."

"Ah. Now we get to it. You want me to loosen up Rose before you interrogate her."

Victoria flipped her hair off her shoulders and raised her chin. "Yes, I do."

From seductive to contrite to bold and pissed. Was it any wonder he couldn't get her out of his mind? "I'll help on one condition." When she nodded, he continued, "What was last night about?"

"Does it have to be about something?"

"I guess not. Were you seducing me then, too? Were you hoping I'd put in a good word for you with Richard?"

"No. You were the one making all the moves, as I recall."

He raised his eyebrows. "Was I?"

Clearly annoyed, she crossed her arms over her chest.

Of course, it only raised her cleavage to new heights, causing a bead of sweat to roll down his back. If he didn't get away from her soon, he was going to wind up promising her anything and everything. "Fine. I'll help."

She laid her hand on his arm. "I'm sorry about, well... this." She glanced down at herself. "Last night was great. It was about you and me and that's all. I know we talked about the contract, but I wasn't thinking about it except those few minutes, and I definitely wasn't considering using you to get to Richard."

"Are you thinking about him now?" Jared linked their hands. "About how fast you can get my cooperation so you can find Rose's necklace and win your contract? About drooling over him the way Peter's been doing all morning?"

"No. Maybe I was earlier, and yuck, no."

"Earlier?"

She swept her hand down her bikini-clad body. "I had a plan."

"What happened to it?"

"I do have some integrity." She sighed when he continued to stare at her. "And when I get close to you I forget all about work and my head goes fuzzy."

He pressed his lips to her forehead. "That's the nicest thing I've heard all day." Sliding his arm around her waist, he led her down the sidewalk toward the pool. "What's for lunch?"

"Gazpacho and sandwiches."

He pictured those little pieces of bread cut into cute triangles. He could eat twenty. "What kind of sandwiches? I'm starving."

"You make your own. Why don't I do that for you while you dote on Rose for a few minutes?"

"Doting is part of my job description."

"I'll bet."

"I'm happy to dote for your cause provided you come out with us this afternoon."

Victoria smiled. "I'm already planning to. How else am I going to interrogate everybody?"

"I didn't misplace my necklace."

With Rose seated at a poolside table between himself and Victoria, Jared wasn't in the position he wanted to be, but he did have genuine concern for his client. "We know."

Rose's hand trembled as she slid it down her iced-tea glass. "Richard assures me you can find it."

Victoria nodded. "I can."

No hesitation. No qualification. No list of the obstacles and potential disasters.

No wonder the woman was at the top of her profession.

Richard didn't deserve her.

Victoria leaned toward Rose and spoke in a low, gentle voice. "In order to recover your jewelry, we need to know your movements last night. From the time you put on the necklace until you locked it in the safe."

"Sure." Rose licked her lips. "I got the necklace out before dinner."

"You unlocked the safe?" Victoria pressed. "You didn't have Mrs. Keegan do it for you?"

Rose shook her head. "I did it. I always do. Richard warned me not to give out the combination to anyone."

"That's smart," Jared said.

"Mrs. Keegan helped me fasten the hook," Rose said. "Then I came downstairs. Everyone saw it at dinner, of course. When the boat ride was suggested, I rushed to my room to take it off. The clasp is old. I really should have it replaced." She toyed with her ham sandwich, which was cut into four tiny triangles. "I'm not as reckless as *some* people might think."

The obvious tension between Richard and his mother was bound to cause Victoria more problems. When Jared got his hands on this thief, he was going to wring his or her neck. What should be a simple weekend enjoying Victoria in a bikini had become a tangled web of motives, hidden agendas and headaches. He knew once Victoria left for Manhattan, he'd never get another chance with her. She'd go back to her life and he to his.

"And the thing is so heavy," Rose added. "My neck was sore."

"So you took it off and put it in the safe?" Victoria asked.

"No, I set it on my dresser."

Victoria glanced significantly at Jared. "Then we all went out on the boat."

"The necklace was unsecured in the house," Jared said.

"Well, yes, but no one else was here," Rose told him.

Victoria nodded. "True. Was the security system on or off?"

"On, I imagine. Though I didn't set it before we left. You'll have to check with Richard or Mrs. Keegan. One of them probably set the property alarm."

"Mrs. K wouldn't take the necklace," Jared felt compelled to point out.

"Of course she wouldn't," Rose agreed. "Besides, it was there when I retired to my room at eleven. Then I put it in the safe. Someone had to have taken it after that." Her throat moved as she swallowed. "While I was asleep."

Creepy, to be sure, but Jared couldn't picture anyone who was staying at the house tiptoeing into Rose's room, accessing the safe—supposedly an intricate feat in itself—then slinking out again. Much less getting back to his or her room without waking anyone or being seen.

The only person with nerves that steely was Victoria, and she'd hardly cause this mess she was now charged with fixing.

Or would she?

If she found the necklace and caught the thief, she'd be Richard's hero. Would she go that far for the contract?

He let his gaze trace the delicate but firm line of her jaw. Her high cheekbones, her clear, perfect eyes.

No. Victoria might be the poster girl for ambition, but she wasn't manipulative. She hadn't been able to hold on to her bikini seduction ruse with him for more than five minutes.

"Where was Sal during that time?" she asked Rose, her voice hushed.

"He slept in a guest room." Rose cleared her throat. "We don't… That is we haven't yet…"

"I'm sorry." Victoria sipped tea, obviously giving Rose a minute to collect herself. "I know it's none of our business."

The woman sighed. "I guess these questions have to be asked. Better you than the police."

So maybe Richard wasn't completely idiotic about not calling the cops, Jared decided. He was being selfish as usual, but his selfishness did have a side benefit for somebody else.

"Do you think we're wrong for not contacting the police, Jared?" Rose asked suddenly, her voice climbing in pitch.

"Yes, but I have confidence in Victoria." He laid his hand over Rose's. "And I'd hate for this to ruin your weekend."

A small smile curved her lips. "Heaven forbid I should miss any of your skiing instructions."

"The activity will be a good distraction for you," Jared said. "Will we have you, too, Victoria?"

By the heat in Victoria's eyes, she didn't miss the double meaning of his words. "Absolutely. I have suspects to grill."

Jared glanced around the pool area, where all the guests were gathered. Mrs. Keegan was refilling glasses of tea and lemonade. The Standishes were seated at an umbrella-shaded table, perched on either side of Richard and looking enraptured by his conversation. Sal and David were still eating lunch. Shelby was serving another bowl of soup to Calla.

One of them was a thief.

Being in the outdoor adventure business, Jared couldn't deny he liked feeling a rush of excitement. Like one of those murder mystery weekend trips, only this plot was real.

"MAKE SURE YOU EASE UP ON THE throttle."

With Jared's deep voice rumbling in her ear, his bare chest pressed against her back and the Jet Ski engine idling beneath her, Victoria's throttle was already in high gear.

She'd watched him do this with other women during the afternoon. Had he pressed himself so intimately against their bodies? Had they tingled in anticipation of more?

The watercraft scooted forward. "See how it's done?" he said loudly over the engine roar and crashing surf.

"I've got it." She twisted the handle so the Jet Ski jolted into motion.

He lifted his hands from hers and wrapped his arms around her. He hadn't done that with the other women. "Easy," he shouted.

"I don't go slow with everything." She grinned. "Today I like fast."

Jared skimmed his lips across her shoulder. "Me, too."

They took off like a shot, parallel to the shoreline, passing Rose and Sal as they putted in the opposite direction on one of the other Jet Skis.

Victoria's friends were right. She needed to relax and get out of Manhattan more.

The ride was exhilarating. The sun warmed her skin as the wind whipped past her ears, tangling her hair. Sea spray splashed over her bare thighs. And a man she'd never seen coming, but couldn't get out of her mind, had a tight grip on her body and her interest.

When she would have turned around to go back, he pointed ahead. "Steer past that big dock. There's a cove."

She slowed the Jet Ski as she rounded the pier, expecting a series of smaller ones tucked into the cove, but there was only sand and a few trees and flowers.

Excitement raced down her spine. Jared hadn't directed them here to point out indigenous fauna.

He stroked her thigh. "I noticed it earlier."

She leaned back against his warm chest and let him take over the steering and guide them into the private cove. With a skill obviously born of long practice, he gunned the engine the last few feet, so the Jet Ski wound up beached.

He held her hand as he helped her climb off. "It'll stay here while we rest." Then, from a center compartment, he pulled out a towel and a small, soft-sided cooler.

Before she could do more than throw him a smile, he'd

laid out the towel and withdrawn two mini champagne bottles from the cooler.

"This towel's pretty small to fit us both," she pointed out.

"We'll have to sit close together then." He lowered himself beside her and tapped his bottle against hers. "To an eventful weekend."

Dragging her gaze away from his broad, muscled chest, she drank, finding the icy champagne soothing to her throat, though her head spun immediately.

Classy, but simple. Which seemed to be Jared's credo.

"This took some planning," she said.

"Mrs. K is a coconspirator," he replied, searching Victoria's gaze as if hoping for approval.

After tucking her snarled hair behind her ear, she reclined on her elbows. She certainly didn't look perfect now, though he didn't seem to care. "Remind me to thank her later."

Jared trailed his finger down her arm. "I will."

She sipped more champagne and forced herself to watch the rolling waves. Her desire to toss aside the bottles and roll on top of him was pretty intense, but he'd let her take command the night before. This was his idea; she'd let him set the pace.

"Thanks for your help with Rose," she said when he remained silent.

"Glad to. I hate to admit Richard might have had a point about not calling the police right away. This would cause not only him but Rose a great deal of embarrassment."

Jared's leg brushed Victoria's, and she squeezed her eyes shut to get control of her lust and concentrate on his words. "I bet the Suffolk County PD is used to being discreet," she managed to say. "Still, I'm not sure we're being entirely lawful."

"Does Shelby know how to make a cake with a file in it? Might come in handy if we need to bust out of jail."

"Shelby can make anything."

"Good to know."

"I should also admit my friends and I have some experience with vigilante justice. Last spring, we headed up Project Robin Hood."

"Robin Hood? The guy in the funny green hat and tights?"

She wrinkled her nose. "No. It's more the spirit of the legend. Righting wrongs. Meting out justice."

"Stealing from the rich to give to the poor?"

Given the nature of the current crime she was solving, she didn't want Jared getting the wrong idea. "Ah...sort of."

She went on to explain the fraud plot she, Calla and Shelby had foiled the previous spring.

"I saw you talking to Peter and Emily, which I guess you wouldn't do without a compelling reason."

"I talked to everybody, and everybody has at least a partial alibi for the hours in question. All the single people were alone for at least a few hours, David for the longest. One of each married couple took a sleeping pill, so the other could have pretended to sleep, then slipped out. But why? Who really has a motive to take the necklace? Who'd risk getting caught?"

"Greed, ambition and the need for money are always popular reasons for just about anything."

"Ambition? How do you mean?"

"Look how clever I am to take this valuable thing without anybody catching me."

"Huh. I could see that, I suppose." The combination of the hot sun, the lulling ocean waves and the champagne relaxed her to the point that she could flip through all the conversations she'd had that day. Plus Jared was so easy to talk to, to share her thoughts with. "I'm not so sure the need for cash is viable with a notorious necklace like that. You couldn't simply pawn it."

"So that leaves greed. A collector?"

She angled her head, considering the idea. "The jealousy story was fascinating, if sad and gruesome."

"But not fascinating enough for you to take the necklace."

"No." She glanced at him. "You?" she asked just as casually.

"Sorry, no."

"Well, that's two down." She paused, thinking about the other guests. "No, four."

"Four?"

"You, me, Calla and Shelby."

"Everybody else is on the suspect list?"

"Have to be, though some seem less likely than others. So it could be a collector, or maybe some kind of compulsion. Like kleptomania. That Emily is an odd little thing."

"Is that a real disease?"

"It is on late-night TV movies." However, Victoria moved psychological trouble to the bottom of the motive list. "It could be an insurance scam. You don't trust Richard's ethics."

"Nope. But Rose doesn't need the money."

Though he'd explained he worked for Rose often, the confidence in his voice was odd. Victoria narrowed her eyes. "How do you know she doesn't need the money?"

"Just a hunch." He shifted his hand to caress her stomach. "You mentioned partial alibis?"

Need crawled through her body at his touch. Did Robin Hood ever have these kinds of conflicts? Sex versus justice? Maybe. Like in the forest when—good grief, she needed to focus. "Nobody can account for every minute during the night, but it's a narrow window. Basically, two till five."

"You and I could have alibied each other."

Her gaze locked with his. "Are you sorry we didn't?"

"It seemed like a gentlemanly thing to do at the time."

"And you care about being a gentleman?"

"Call me old-fashioned, but yes."

"Do you care about the theft of the necklace?"

His eyes blazed. "Not right now."

Setting her bottle and his in the sand, he kissed her, his tongue immediately tangling with hers, driving her desire to new heights.

As his arm encircled her, he held her against his bare chest. The heat of their bodies came together, creating an inferno of sensation. Victoria wished she could blame her breathlessness on the Jet Ski or the sun, but she knew Jared alone had such an affect on her.

He trailed kisses down her neck, and she clutched at him. She shouldn't want him this badly, after so short a time knowing him…barely twenty-four hours. But she could hardly argue with her body when it so clearly knew what it wanted.

When he cupped her breast, she couldn't fight back a moan. Dipping his thumb beneath the bare scrap of her bathing suit top, he glided it back forth over her nipple, shooting sparks of need over her skin.

Spearing her hand through his silky hair, she urged his mouth back to hers. She kissed him in appreciation and encouragement. She'd never had sex in the sand, much less outdoors, but he was the king of adventure. When in Rome…

Pressing her back, he hovered over her, his handsome face flushed. "You know I want you."

She couldn't mistake his erection against her side. She licked her lips. "I want you, too."

"But I don't want to consummate our relationship here. There are a lot of people on the water. Anybody could come by."

She drew a deep breath in an effort to get control of her racing heart. "Good point."

When he helped her to her feet, she smiled. "Consummate? You are old-fashioned."

"Problem?"

"It's sweet." She slid her finger down his chest. "And I could use sweet. My love life is…"

"Boring?" he prompted in a hopeful voice.

"Corporate," she admitted.

"Not everything's about the art of the deal."

She looked into his warm, brown eyes, and for the first

time in recent memory believed in tenderness and happily ever after.

Robin had known what he was fighting for. Did she?

9

WHILE THE REST OF THE houseguests were in their quarters changing for dinner, Victoria invited Calla and Shelby to her room for cocktails.

Calla raised her glass. "To Jared McKenna in a swimsuit."

"I'll drink to that," Victoria said, tapping crystal against Calla's.

"Me, too," Shelby declared. When the other two looked at her in surprise, she shrugged. "Hey, I'm engaged, not blind."

As they enjoyed their drinks, Victoria recalled the sight of Jared walking out of the surf, scooping back his wavy dark hair, the muscles in his chest and shoulders flexing, his teeth flashing white against his tanned face.

Like an island vacation ad. A great one.

"One of us has better memories than the others," Calla commented slyly.

Victoria looked around to find her friends staring at her. "Yeah." Warmth spread through her that had nothing to do with her martini. "One of us does."

"Details," Shelby demanded.

Victoria leaned back in her chair. "Some of us got a Jet Ski ride that others didn't."

"A literal ride?" Shelby asked.

"You're already having sex with him?" Calla asked at the same time.

"Yes, a literal ride. No to sex." Though Victoria imagined the possibilities. "We have plans to correct that later."

"How romantic," Calla said sarcastically. "You managed to fit him in your schedule."

"Hey." Victoria poked her friend's knee. "It's not like I put the event down in my digital calendar. I thought it was very romantic of him to not settle for a fast grope in the sand."

Shelby groaned. "I'd settle for any kind of grope from Trevor."

Calla rolled her eyes. "You've been away from him for one night."

"It's a holiday weekend," Shelby said. "We had plans."

"You can reschedule your Between the Sheets Symposium," Calla assured her.

Victoria met each of her friends' gaze in turn. "I know you guys would rather be someplace else."

"No." Shelby made an effort to bring herself back into focus. "This is a good booking for me. Trevor and I will have a lifetime of weekends."

"I got some great shots today," Calla said. "And Rose told me she'd like some pictures of the house's interior tomorrow. I think I'll have a sellable piece for *Coastal Life*." Her eyes lit with promise. "Not to mention we have a real-life mystery on our hands. Maybe I could work on that for *Fiction Monthly*."

"As the recently appointed Robin Hood of the group, I'd like to point out crime solving isn't as easy as it looks." Victoria recounted her conversations with the other guests about their movements during the night. "David was alone for the longest stretch of time, followed by Rose and Sal, but the timeline allows for basically anybody to steal the necklace."

"But not the knowledge," Calla argued. "Seems to me Richard and Rose, and maybe Ruthie, are the only ones who could've gotten into that safe."

"Does Ruthanne even have the combination?" Victoria asked the group in general.

"I still think Sal has shifty eyes," Shelby said.

Dismissing Sal's eyes, Victoria leaned back, crossing her legs as she considered the only theory that, to her, made sense. "I'm wondering if this is an insurance scam. But when I mentioned that to Jared, he said Rose has plenty of money."

"How does Jared know about Rose's finances?" Shelby asked, frowning.

"Exactly what I wanted to know," Victoria returned. "He said he had a hunch, so I figure he meant the opulence of this place. But she wouldn't be the first socialite to appear wealthy and instead be in debt up to her fake, diamond-studded earrings."

Calla drank the last of her lemon drop, then set the glass on the table. "I saw this movie once where some rich chick had sold her diamond necklace to pay off gambling debts, and had a paste copy made so her husband wouldn't find out. Then one day he announces he wants to add some stones to the necklace."

Shelby grinned. "Oops."

"No kidding," Calla agreed. "Anyway, she hired some guy to break into her house and steal the jewelry."

"You think Rose could be that devious?" Victoria asked.

"Anybody's capable of anything, given the right motivation." Shelby lifted her glass. "Look at our track record."

"At least we had police support when we caught that creep who'd swindled Shelby's parents," Calla pointed out. "I don't like keeping this a secret."

Shelby shook her head. "It's never going to stay secret."

"Agreed," Victoria added. But she'd promised Richard, so for now, at least, they were stuck solving the mystery themselves.

Victoria had barely completed the thought when Calla leaned forward, looking determined. "I think we need help."

"From who?" she asked, though she knew.

"Devin, of course."

"No," Victoria said. "No way. I told Richard I could handle this. The necklace has been missing for less than twelve hours. Give me some time."

"We're breaking the law by not reporting the theft," Calla argued.

Though Victoria had thought the same thing, she didn't want to be reminded of her conscience just now. "How do you know?"

Calla lifted her chin. "I know."

Victoria scowled. "You just want to talk to Devin."

"I'd rather see him," Calla said, unrepentant. "You think he'd like a ride on a Jet Ski?"

"I don't see how we can invite somebody to Rose's house without asking her," Shelby said. "Especially an NYPD detective."

Calla wasn't deterred. "He can go undercover, be Jared's assistant or something."

"This doesn't seem like Devin's kind of place," Shelby said gently.

"We need help," Calla repeated.

Victoria surged to her feet. "Are you out of your mind? If we call the cops, I lose the contract. End of discussion."

Silence permeated the room. Victoria's control was slipping away. The perfect vision of her corner office wavered and faded, becoming so indistinct she wasn't sure she could ever regain focus.

Her friends were right, and she was wrong. Although that didn't lessen her desire to win.

"I'm sorry, V," Shelby said in a low voice. "But Calla's right about one thing. We do need legal advice."

"We could call your dad," Calla suggested.

Victoria shook her head. "No way am I dragging him into this. Besides, he's a corporate lawyer. How would he know about police procedure?"

"So we're back to Devin," Calla said.

Victoria didn't see the moody detective being any more inclined to help than her father. "If we call him and tell him about the theft, he'll definitely have to report it."

"So we'll be hypothetical," Calla offered, already pulling her cell phone from the back pocket of her jeans. "We'll ask for a generic opinion."

That would never work. "He'll know something's up."

Calla let out a delighted laugh. "That'll be half the fun."

Before Victoria could come up with another excuse to escape this bad idea, Calla had laid her cell phone on the coffee table. Through the speakerphone, everyone could hear the line ringing.

"Antonio," Devin said, his deep voice hoarse.

"Hi. It's Calla Tucker." She frowned. "You sound terrible."

"I'm hungover," the detective grumbled.

"Sorry," Calla said brightly—whether because she'd gotten her way or because she was talking to the object of her crush, Victoria wasn't sure. "I've got you on speakerphone with Victoria and Shelby."

Dead silence from the detective. Then he growled, "What the hell are the three of you into now?"

Calla pushed out her lower lip, looking for all the world like a beauty queen who'd lost her crown. "Why would you think that?"

"Wild guess," he said.

"Some friend you are." She huffed out an annoyed breath. "I just called to see how you were doing."

"You called to see how I'm doing," he echoed slowly.

Victoria could all but see the combination of frustration, aggravation and lust on his striking face.

"Yeah." Calla played with the stem of her cocktail glass. "We could chat."

"Is this some kind of joke?"

"No."

"You heard me say I'm hungover."

"Yes."

"So is this some kind of joke?"

Victoria exchanged a pained expression with Shelby. The man was undeniably difficult.

Shelby leaned toward the phone. "Detective, it's Shelby Dixon. We actually called to ask your advice about a point of law."

"So phone a lawyer," he suggested, surly as ever. "I hear there are a couple million in Manhattan."

"I'm sure there are," Shelby answered, "but we're not in the city. We're at a weekend house party in Southampton. We have a question." Noticing Calla's frantically waving hands, Shelby added, "Like a trivia question. Is it a crime not to report a crime when it's committed?"

More silence.

"Please, Detective," Shelby added, "it's important."

"Yeah, yeah," he answered finally. "Depending on the seriousness of the crime, and the players involved, you can get accessory after the fact. That's a general charge for helping somebody get away with criminal activity."

"But we don't want the criminal to get away," Calla said.

"Then why…" He stopped, heaving a deep sigh. "Damn. The gang is on the loose again."

"We're not a gang," they said together.

"Practice that line for when the judge adds a conspiracy charge," he retorted.

"What did you mean, 'the players involved'?" Victoria asked, preferring not to imagine that courtroom scenario.

"Public officials, teachers and government employees are held to a higher standard than the general public when it comes to concealing crimes. They can be charged with obstruction of justice, which is much more serious than being an accessory after the fact."

"How could a judge charge us with conspiracy?" Victoria asked, since that was exactly what was going on in this crazy house.

"Are you complicit? Did you help the perpetrator get away with the crime—before or after the act itself?"

They didn't intend to let the thief get away, but if they compromised the evidence and scene of the crime—which, given her and Mrs. K's poking around, they'd already done—that could ultimately happen. The whole business was growing more complicated and dangerous by the hour.

Still, "accessory after the fact" didn't sound so bad. At least not bad enough to land them in prison.

"Ms. Holmes," the detective said, breaking into her thoughts, "have you committed a crime?"

"No."

"Has anyone in the room with you right now committed a crime?"

"No." Victoria paused, but forged ahead after a frantic nod by Calla. "We're playing a trivia game. All purely innocent."

"Would you say I'm the least gullible person you know?" the detective asked.

Victoria felt no satisfaction in admitting she'd been right about this plan having no chance of working. "You're certainly in the top three. But we'd like to ask you about a personal matter."

Calla's eyes widened. This time she gave Victoria a vigorous head shake. Good grief, not *that* personal.

Ignoring Calla's panic attack, Victoria asked Devin, "Could you do a financial background investigation of a friend? Her name is Rose Rutherford."

"I know that name."

"She owns the house we're staying in."

"Then I'd say her financial background is pretty solid. Have a nice day."

"Don't hang up," Calla begged. "We need help."

"Sure thing," he replied, his tone biting. "I can spend my morning working for you guys. We're just skipping through the meadow around here at the NYPD. Not a single piece of paper on anyone's desk. Not a phone has rung all morning.

Criminals seem to have taken the day off." He paused meaningfully. "Except for your gang, of course."

"We're not a gang," they all said automatically.

"Glad to hear it. Let me know who wins the game."

They exchanged frustrated glances. It seemed undeniably arrogant and selfish of them to expect the detective to do their research. That was Richard's way. But Victoria had hung her promotion hopes around his neck.

"Please, Devin," Calla finally said, her voice soft.

If that didn't do it...

Antonio sighed. "Okay, fine. Whatever. I'll see what I can find out. But I think you're wasting your time. The Rutherfords are loaded."

"While you're looking into her, would you check out a few more people?" Calla asked sweetly, then listed the names of everyone at the house party, including Jared and Mrs. Keegan.

Though Victoria instinctively doubted either of the last two on Calla's list was guilty, she guessed it couldn't hurt to be thorough. Maybe if they presented all their findings to the sheriff, he wouldn't be so quick to arrest them for accessory, conspiracy or in general being stupid enough to think they could be better cops than the cops.

"Anything else?" the detective asked. "I live to serve."

"We really appreciate this," Shelby said. "Next week I'll bring by some of those chocolate peanut butter cookies you like so much."

He grunted, apparently his idea of gratitude.

"Drink lots of water and orange juice," Calla advised.

"Or a Bloody Mary," Shelby added. "Though if you're on duty, a Virgin Mary. And get some rest."

"Yeah, sure," Antonio said. "I've had hangovers before."

Victoria made a mental note to make a donation to the Law Enforcement Memorial Fund. Cookies were a comfort, but she didn't cook, and she did have plenty of money.

Just before Calla pressed the button to disconnect the call, his voice rose from the speaker. "You three didn't kill any-body, did you?"

"No," they said in unison.

"Why don't I believe you?"

PLAYING BARTENDER AT RICHARD'S urging, Jared glanced toward the living-room doorway for what had to be the twentieth time.

Where is she?

Everyone else had already arrived for cocktail hour and were happily sipping drinks. After his and Victoria's afternoon at the beach, his need to be with her had multiplied a hundredfold. Even during his cold shower, he hadn't been able to block the vision of her toned body in that yellow bikini. Or the desire-filled smile on her face as she'd leaned toward him for a kiss.

After again noticing the empty doorway, he reached into the minifridge for a beer. He'd bet his prize heifer her lateness had something to do with that damn necklace and Richard's burden of making her promise to find it.

He sipped and watched the guests gather by the bar. Shelby was passing around a tray of appetizers, while the others had conversations in duos and trios.

Peter, as usual, was rambling on to Richard. "The atmosphere at Coleman PR is competitive, of course, but most of us thrive on pressure. It's just who we are."

Rose was telling David about spending the afternoon fielding calls from neighbors, excited about the party planned for the following night.

"I was a high school science teacher before I met Peter," he heard Emily say to Calla. "Now all I seem to do is throw dinner parties for his clients."

Speaking of dinner…tonight's menu was something to look forward to. He was starving, so veal medallions, twice-baked potatoes and grilled asparagus sounded like—

He halted as Victoria strode into the room.

She wore a body-hugging white dress and sky-high gold shoes with needlelike heels that made Jared break out in a cold sweat. She looked left, then right, hesitating when she saw Peter and Richard. Ultimately, though, she headed straight toward Jared. "You're working hard today."

Predictably, thanks to her nearness, his heart thrummed wildly in his chest. "I sort of volunteered."

She raised her eyebrows, perfectly arched over her crystal blue eyes.

"After Richard suggested I volunteer."

She let out a delighted laugh that made every muscle in Jared's body come to attention. "Seems I'm not the only one vulnerable to suggestion."

"I'm up for anything you've got."

"Same goes."

He leaned over the bar. "How about a boat ride after dinner?" he whispered.

"We did that last night."

"Nobody but you and me are invited tonight."

"Sounds…private."

"That's the idea." He pulled a frosted glass from the icebox, then flipped it. "Very cold vodka martini, straight up, two olives?" When she looked surprised, he added, "Shelby told me."

"Nice," Victoria said after her first sip.

He noted a sparkling ring on her middle finger that hadn't been there the night before. It was delicate, unlike Rose's over-the-top necklace, and suited Victoria flawlessly.

"What did I miss this afternoon after I went inside?" she asked. "Anybody confess to taking the necklace?"

"Sorry, no. What were you and your friends doing closed up in your room?"

She gave him a long study. "Girl talk."

"About me or the thief?"

"Some of both. You're curious."

"You're vague. And they came down long before you did.

Are you one of those women who take forever to get ready for everything?"

She paused with her glass halfway to her mouth. "One of *those* women?"

"Yeah, you know, ones who're primping and changing clothes all the time. I like to know what I'm getting into."

"Right now, you're putting your private boat ride in serious jeopardy."

He held up his hands in surrender. "Kidding. I'm only kidding."

"Well, cut it out. I'm one of those women who aren't the butt of jokes very often."

"Really? Why?"

"I know you may find this hard to believe, but I intimidate a lot of people."

He stroked the back of her hand. "Not to worry. Us adventurers are a tough lot."

"Good to know." She sipped her drink. "Did Emily ever get up on the skis?"

He'd been expecting Victoria to turn around and frown over Peter monopolizing Richard, so it took him a second to process her question. "No, but neither did Richard." He retrieved his beer from under the counter. "The surf was rough."

"So I noticed."

"You did pretty well." He paused, but couldn't resist needling her again. "For a city girl."

She nudged his arm. "A city girl who spends her fair share of time at the gym."

"I could tell you didn't get your body by sitting in a boardroom."

"You, too. Though with your job, I imagine staying in shape is a requirement."

"It helps. But my job's not the only thing—"

"Victoria," Richard said as he approached, "I was wondering where you were. Peter seems to be everywhere."

Jared squeezed his beer bottle so tightly he was surprised it didn't shatter.

Victoria showed no such emotion, though Jared imagined she felt the same way. Her gaze flicked to her rival. "I've always thought Peter was amazingly agile."

He was slippery, all right. Victoria was running around solving Richard's problems, while he let Peter fawn over him and think he had a chance at the contract. Which he didn't. As long as Victoria found that cursed necklace…

Jared resented the whole damn situation, and didn't like Richard compromising everybody's ethics in order to save his reputation. Jared didn't care a whit whether those gems were in somebody's suitcase or at the bottom of the sea. But he was going to do everything in his power to make sure Victoria found the thief and got her precious contract.

Even though he'd much rather see Richard fall on his pampered ass.

Peter captured Victoria's hand and brushed his lips over the back of it, while Jared clenched his jaw. "We have to use the talents given to us," Peter said. "Not everyone has Victoria's looks and designer wardrobe to fall back on."

A flicker of resentment darted through Victoria's eyes.

And for good reason. With Peter implying her beauty and family money were the reason for her success, it was no wonder she wanted to beat him so badly.

"Those classes in grooming and fashion at Harvard have really come in handy," she said, her tone packed with sarcasm.

Richard, possibly sensing Victoria was on the verge of crushing Peter beneath her stiletto, handed Jared his empty tumbler. "How about a refill? I can't imagine what's holding up dinner."

Jared would be happy to play bartender for hours. Maybe tipsy guests would lead to a confession.

But he'd just handed Richard the fresh drink when Mrs. K appeared in the doorway and announced the meal.

As everyone wandered into the dining room, Jared made

sure he walked next to Victoria. "I take it Peter doesn't have an Ivy League diploma?" he said close to her ear.

"If he has a degree at all, it's probably mail order."

But was he clever or desperate enough to snatch a valuable necklace from right under their noses?

And if so, why?

10

As DESSERT WAS BEING SERVED, Rose stood and tapped her spoon against her wineglass. "I have an exciting announcement."

You found that stupid, ostentatious necklace that's keeping Victoria from fully enjoying the important things this weekend. Such as me.

Jared's selfish thought was doomed to remain unfulfilled, he realized when Rose declared, "We're adding costumes to the party tomorrow night!"

Seated across from him, Victoria gave her hostess a strained smile before her gaze locked with his. *What's this bunch of bull?* he could imagine her saying.

And he doubted anybody at the table besides Rose thought costumes were a good idea.

"That's a marvelous suggestion, Mother," Richard said, clearly amused. "But I left my superhero cape back in the city."

"Not to worry." Rose was practically bouncing with delight. "I have all the costumes in the attic. They're premier fashions from the 1920s. I've been saving them forever, and there are plenty to choose from for men and women. It's going to be such fun."

Only Ruthie was brave enough to say what everybody else was no doubt thinking. "You want us all to wear a bunch of old clothes that have been sitting in the dusty attic for ninety years?"

Rose let out a huff. "They may be *vintage,* but they're not dusty. They've been pristinely preserved in airtight bags and a cedar trunk. Our lovely dinner party tomorrow night will be dedicated to the memory of my necklace, the stones of which were mined during those jovial years." She gave a dramatic sniff. "I might never get it back, you know."

"How are all the neighbors going to come up with costumes on such short notice?" Richard asked.

For once, Jared was grateful to hear his opinion.

"They won't be wearing them," Rose explained. "I have only enough for us. We're the hosts."

As she beamed, Jared mentally reviewed his contract. He was pretty positive costume-wearing wasn't mentioned anywhere.

Unfortunately, before anybody could voice another objection, Rose turned to Shelby. "Do you think you can make a historically inspired meal?"

Shelby looked a bit startled to be put on the spot, and was probably wondering how she was going to change the menu with less than a day's notice, but she nodded. "I'm sure I can come up with something."

"Great." Rose beamed. "It's settled. Remember, cocktails and hors d'oeuvres start at six." She turned to Sal. "Would you mind helping me and Mrs. Keegan bring down the costumes from the attic?"

"I need to check my email," Richard said, surging to his feet. "I'll see all of you in the morning."

The other guests also suddenly professed vital plans. Obviously, no one wanted to spend the rest of the night sorting through old clothes, no matter how well preserved. Jared could hardly blame them. The next pile of clothes he wanted to see were his and Victoria's, tossed on the floor.

Peter stretched dramatically. "I'm beat. Come on, Emily. Let's turn in."

His wife looked as if she was going to argue. It was barely ten o'clock after all. Throwing her husband a resentful glare, she pushed herself to her feet and followed him from the room.

Shelby, Calla and Ruthie headed off toward the kitchen, chattering about wanting to see the pictures Calla had taken during the day, which she'd copied to her laptop. David was recruited to help Sal and Rose.

In a few miraculous minutes, Jared and Victoria were alone. He rocked back on his heels. "So, Ms. Holmes, what would you like to do?"

Victoria made a show of considering her options. "How about a boat ride?" she finally suggested.

He offered his arm. "I'm at your service."

The landscape lighting illuminated the sidewalk, dock and pool area, casting an ethereal glow on the trees swaying in the ocean breeze. As mood setter, it was perfect.

She slipped off her heels when they reached the dock. "Using costumes at a dinner party as a coping mechanism for losing a priceless necklace is pretty strange, don't you think?"

"Better than sitting in a dark corner with a bottle of whiskey."

"True. So we all get to look ridiculous instead."

"Everybody but you and me."

She cast a sideways glance at him. "How are we going to get out of it?"

"I doubt any of the clothes will be large enough to fit me." He jumped onto the boat, then extended his hand to help her aboard. "And you could never look ridiculous no matter what you're wearing."

"Sometimes you say the nicest things."

"Sometimes?"

"A lot of the time."

"I'm trying to impress you." He squeezed her hand. "Let's get going. I have a theory I want to run by you."

"You want to talk about the theft?" she asked in a tone that told him she definitely didn't.

But since what he wanted to do was peel that dress off her as quickly as possible, he figured talking about the necklace would distract him long enough to get his baser impulses under control. At least until the yacht was well away from the estate.

He untied it from the dock, then helped her up the ladder to the captain's perch, where he got them under way before broaching the subject of the missing jewelry. "You said Peter took a sleeping pill before bed last night," Jared began.

"That's what he said."

"He could've lied."

"You honestly think Peter is the thief?" she asked in surprise, shaking her head. "He doesn't have the creativity. Or the brains."

"What if he took the necklace so he could 'find' it and be the big hero to Richard?"

"He's going to suddenly pull it from the sofa cushions? And what about Rose saying she locked it in the safe? How's Peter going to explain how it got from there to wherever he's going to find it?"

"He won't if he's smart. 'Hey, look what I found.' Leave it at that."

"Leaving the thief unidentified."

"If the necklace is back, safe and sound, who would care? Rose could add the mystery into her next themed dinner party, and everybody else would assume she'd been mistaken about locking it in the safe."

"It's a good plan," Victoria agreed, tucking her windblown hair behind her ears. "Certainly one you could think of. Peter? Not so much."

Jared recalled Peter bragging about his knowledge of horses, talking about the Thoroughbreds he'd ridden at a Montana spa—even though a Thoroughbred's skinny legs were designed for speed at Churchill Downs and would likely snap over the first rocky patch of western terrain. "Yeah. I see your point."

Frankly, he didn't see anyone, besides Victoria and her friends, capable of pulling off such a bold theft. David seemed too polite, Emily too high-strung. Nobody knew Sal well. Shelby had tried to convince him Rose's companion had shifty eyes, but he'd seemed okay to Jared. Good-natured, in fact. Which any man would have to be to endure Rose's tendency toward drama. Could he really—

Dude, what are you doing, obsessing about that ridiculous necklace when a woman as sexy as Victoria is within touching distance?

He studied her. Her shoes discarded on the deck, she was curled up in the corner of the sofa near the wheel, with her face turned into the wind, inky hair blowing back from her gorgeous face. "You're sitting awfully far away," he said.

Smiling, she patted the empty space beside her. "There's plenty of room." She angled her head. "Is there a remote control for this thing?"

He rose from the captain's chair and extended one hand, clasping the wheel with the other. "I can still keep it between the channel markers."

She stood in front of him and he embraced her from behind, inhaling the flowery scent of her hair. "It's quiet out here," she said. "Almost eerie. I'm used to the noise of Manhattan."

He rubbed his lips against the soft skin beneath her ear. "The noises in nature are better."

"Like crickets and birds?"

"Sure, but I was thinking more like the sound of heavy breathing." He stroked her stomach. "A fast beating heart."

She dropped her head against his chest. "That's a good sound."

He trailed slow, lingering kisses down her neck, while keeping his hand moving across her stomach. When she let out a low moan, he dipped his fingers between her legs. Even through her dress, he could feel her heat. Could feel her responding to his touch, wanting more.

She pressed her backside to his erection, and he held her there. The pressure was heavenly. Yet he needed so much more. The realization that he was going to get more, to possess this remarkable woman, even for a little while, honed the sharpness of his desire.

She turned, looping her arms around his neck. "How are we going to do this without wrecking the boat?"

"I know a quiet cove where we can drop the anchor."

"Condoms?"

"In my pocket."

She flicked her tongue over his earlobe, causing his heart to hammer faster. "I do like a man who's prepared."

WHILE JARED WAS DEALING WITH the anchor, Victoria headed into the main cabin. The bedroom was located in the stern. Decorated in a kitschy nautical theme, the room boasted a king-size bed with a plush navy comforter.

Handy. They'd use every inch of it.

She giggled at the idea as she sat at the end.

Hold it. *Giggling?* What the hell was wrong with her? She couldn't be nervous. She didn't get nervous.

What was really so special about this moment, this guy?

On the surface, he was all a woman would ever want— strong, smart, good-looking. But there was something deeper, something meaningful in the way her heart pounded when she saw him or touched him. His honesty was a balm to the sometimes back-stabbing world she lived in.

Or heard him, she realized, as his footsteps echoed down the hall, and her pulse picked up speed.

"Hi," he said, his large frame filling the tiny doorway.

"H-hi," she croaked out, then winced, knowing she'd betrayed her anxiety.

He sat beside her and cupped her cheek tenderly. "You okay?"

Oh, yeah.

Apprehension vanished. "Come closer," she said, her gaze roving his rugged features.

He leaned in until his face was inches away.

"A little closer," she whispered.

His mouth immediately connected with hers.

Perfect.

She breathed in his woodsy, masculine scent, and a needy ache spread through her belly. She angled her head as his tongue caressed hers, and clutched his shirt in her fists, wanting his body on hers, inside hers.

With his hands at her waist, he lay back, pulling her with him. She liked having him beneath her, leaving her free to explore his powerful frame, to learn where he liked to be touched, what strokes made him moan.

Her fingers trembled as she unbuttoned his shirt. She knew how beautiful his chest was. She recalled running her palms over his heated skin on the beach earlier that day, and repeated the caress now. He clutched her tighter against him, slipping his hands into her hair.

His heart beat as quickly as hers, but he let her set the pace. She left a trail of kisses down his throat and across his chest. He had muscles she didn't know the human body possessed, and a tiny scar on his shoulder that she touched the tip of her tongue to.

He sucked in a ragged breath and shifted his hands to the hem of her dress, inching it up her body. She lifted off him long enough for him to tug it over her head, then straddled him, the heat between her legs pressed intimately to his washboard stomach.

His gaze tracked down her body, clearly approving of the skimpy, nude-colored bra and panty set she wore. "Beautiful," he said, his tone low and hungry.

He slid his palms up her sides, then cupped her breasts, flicking his thumbs over her nipples.

She closed her eyes as desire overlook her, sending ripples of burning need through her blood. Rolling her hips, she pressed the growing dampness of her body against his skin. She couldn't remember the last time she'd let go like this— the last time she'd enjoyed heat and intimacy more than bodies simply satisfying an urge.

He reared up, fusing his mouth to hers. She wrapped her arms around his neck and echoed his surge of passion. His erection rubbed her center, and through the bits of cloth they wore, she tingled, then caught on fire, knowing she would climax the instant he touched her.

Either he sensed her thoughts, or his own need was too great to ignore any longer, because he lifted her off him and got rid of his pants. Victoria mirrored his moves, divesting herself of her lingerie and tossing it to the floor.

Naked, he tugged her to the bed, where he quickly dealt with protection before urging her on top of him.

Victoria was sure she should say something, something teasing and sexy, but her body throbbed, demanding satisfaction, in no mood to argue about aesthetics.

She poised herself above his erection and sank down in one powerful stroke.

As expected, she did climax, letting out a rapturous sigh as her inner walls pulsed around him. With her hands positioned on either side of his head, she braced herself, while ripples of pleasure reverberated down her spine. He arched his body into hers, going, if possible, even deeper inside her.

"Damn, V," he moaned.

She kissed him deeply in appreciation and anticipation, since he was still hard as steel and she knew more bliss lay ahead for them.

Straightening, she glided her palms over his chest and began to rock her hips. His hands clenched her thighs. She felt strong and powerful, giving him the strokes he craved, and her movements had the itch of need in her own body flickering back to life.

His hands moved across her skin, hot and sure. He captured her nipples between his thumbs and fingers, stimulating a hunger that shot down her abdomen and pulsed between her legs. She bit her bottom lip as the ache spread.

She couldn't remember ever being so in sync with a man. The first time was generally spotted with tentative touches, fumbling or learning the right rhythm. Was Jared so superior a lover, or were they truly well matched?

He jolted her from her thoughts when he reached up and sank his teeth lightly into her left nipple.

Smiling at her surprise, he gripped the back of her head, then flipped them. She immediately hooked her legs around his waist. He thrust inside her, retreated, then pushed inside again. She could see the intense need stamped on his face. He was through with teasing. His heart-pounding pace was about outright need and seduction.

She arched her back as his thrusts became shorter and quicker. His breath covered her cheek and she wanted more than anything to please him, to show him how quickly he'd become a solace for all the turmoil surrounding them. Beads of sweat clotted her burning face. *Almost there...*

Hung at the edge, she dug her fingernails into the sheets.

Then he teased her once more, and she climaxed.

He followed her in seconds, moaning deep in his throat, holding her tight as the pulses undulated through her and the waves rocked around them.

LYING ON HIS BACK BESIDE Victoria, Jared gasped for air.

Tremors of ecstasy continued to pulse through his body. He couldn't imagine when, if ever, he'd felt so amazing.

Scuba diving in the Caymans?

No.

Skiing in Jackson Hole?

No.

Hang gliding in Rio?

Not even then.

She scooted closer, resting her cheek on his chest, tangling their bare legs. He stroked her silky hair, kissed the top of her head.

Being right here was too great to consider being anywhere else. He'd never pictured Victoria cuddling contently next to him, as if he was the only thing on her mind. He'd always figured she had a million thoughts going on in her brain at once.

She slid her hand across his chest, her mouth following the same path. Her hot breath caressed his skin, and when her lips brushed his earlobe, his heart jumped.

Suddenly she propped herself up on her elbow, meeting his gaze. "Did you call me V?"

Okay, a million and one. He struggled to think back. "Maybe."

"I thought you said it wasn't an imaginative nickname."

"It's not."

"So?"

What answer would get her lips back on his body? "Well… my imagination wasn't exactly…engaged."

"I think other parts were engaged." Smiling, she pressed her lips to his jaw. "For the record, I like V. Especially when you say it in that breathy way you did earlier."

He glided his fingers down her back. "I still think Tori is fun." He paused, recalling what she'd said. "I'm a guy. I don't do breathy."

She shrugged. "You're the one who called it out in the heat of passion."

He wrapped his arms around her and rolled so he hovered over her. "A man will say anything in the heat of passion."

Lifting her hand, she stroked his face, her eyes shimmering like pure blue pools of water. "Not you. You only say what you mean."

"Let's go back to the house."

"There are lots of people at the house."

"I bet we can find a room or two that's empty. Besides, there's the leisurely ride back."

SEATED IN THE CAPTAIN'S CHAIR and trying to keep his hand steady on the steering wheel, Jared let out a needy groan. Victoria wore nothing. He had on his pants. Unbuttoned, as she was currently sitting on his left thigh and running her hand up and down the hardened length of his penis.

They puttered as slowly as possible along the Atlantic shoreline. He didn't trust his powers of concentration even in the deserted waters.

"I can't believe we're doing this," he said.

She pressed a lingering kiss to his shoulder. "One of your better ideas."

As she shifted her position, his muscles tensed. The woman had an incredible touch.

When she straddled him, her thighs on either side of his, rubbing her warm center against his erection, he closed his eyes to keep control.

He was torn between wanting to drive himself inside her and letting the pleasure go on endlessly. They were compatible in investigating and lovemaking. And though he was still uncomfortable with keeping secrets—especially from cops—he had secrets of his own, so he could hardly judge.

"Don't you want to watch?" she said against his ear.

His eyes popped open and his thoughts scattered.

With a teasing smile on her beautiful face, she reached into his back pocket and pulled out a condom. Slowly, she stuck the corner of the packet in her mouth and tore it open with her teeth.

Oh, man.

His erection pulsed in time with his heart. She paused in her stroking only long enough to roll on the protection.

"We're not going to hit the shore, are we?"

"What shore?" he asked, an instant before he jerked his attention to the course the boat was taking, cutting through the black water. Thankfully, the shore was still on his right and the vast sea on his left.

"You drive," she said, lifting her body to the tip of his erection. "I'll do all the work."

She moved down, inch by excruciating inch, until he was seated deep in her core. Grasping his shoulders, she threw her head back and rolled her hips forward. Sparks of ecstasy caught fire and shot through every cell of his body.

With an intensely grateful sigh, she rocked against him, her rhythm lazy and steady at first, but increasing in tempo, along with her breathing. He let her take her pleasure as she wished, thrilled to be her partner.

His plan to change her mind about the kind of men who interested her was working. So why did he feel like a fraud? To quiet his conscience, he stroked her silky thigh. Her hardened nipples grazed his chest, sending lightning pulses shooting across his skin.

A whimper started in the back of her throat, telling him she was near climax. She dug her fingertips into his shoulders. Driven by her growing demand, he worked against her, matching her speed and intensity.

As his own peak approached, he cut the boat's throttle and threw his arms around her, glorying in the satisfaction he could feel drawing near, in the summit just out of reach.

His orgasm surged before he was ready, but his triggered hers. Her body fluttered around him, squeezing and releasing, drawing out his rapture. She ground herself deeper as the contractions subsided, and he pressed a clinging kiss to her throat.

As she tucked her head between his neck and shoulder, he fought to breathe.

And steer.

Even without the engine engaged, the yacht chopped through the waves. Boats didn't have brakes, after all.

"I really like being on top," she gasped.

"So I see."

She moved enough to kiss him, her tongue gliding against

his, her passion sated but certainly not gone. "I haven't enjoyed myself so much in a long time," she said.

"Me, either."

"Not just sex-wise," she added. "I mean, I like being with you, talking to you."

"You don't usually talk to your lovers?"

"I give them a bottle of water before I shove them out the door."

The unexpectedly vulnerable expression on her face made Jared question his happiness about being right from the beginning.

He'd wanted her when they met, and he'd done everything he could to have her. But now that he held her, where were they? Where would they go?

They had careers and lives to continue when the weekend was over.

A career you lied about, by the way.

And yet here, with her heart beating against his, this is what seemed truly important.

Sighing, she snuggled against him once more with her head on his chest, a position he wouldn't have imagined her enjoying when they'd met. Was he the difference?

She stroked his neck. "Where'd you go?"

Dragging himself back to reality, he had no tangible explanation for the exhilaration in his heart. He bordered on giddy.

And he didn't do giddy.

His family would check him into the nearest mental health clinic if he even said the word *giddy,* unless it was immediately followed by *up.*

"I'm trying to get us back on course," he said, cranking the engine. "We'll wind up drifting to Europe."

"Fine by me," she murmured, spearing her fingers through his hair.

Right. Then she'd never forgive him when Richard woke up and she wasn't there to make everything in his life perfect. "I'll take you some other time," he said.

As the words came out of his mouth, he regretted them. She no doubt considered their liaison was only for the weekend. Beyond that, they had little in common.

"I should probably have clothes on when we get back to the house," she said, moving off his lap. She kissed him lightly, then found her discarded dress and undies.

After getting dressed—a damn shame, in his opinion—she brought him his shirt and helped him slide his arms into the sleeves. Returning to her perch on his knee, she placed a tender kiss in the center of his chest before doing up the buttons.

The whole scene was unnerving, yet comforting, as if they'd done this together a thousand times.

They rode the rest of the way to the estate in silence, with her head resting on his shoulder, his arm tucked around her.

When they reached the dock, she nimbly leaped onto it and caught the rope Jared threw her, so they could guide the boat into its slip. With the ties secured, they strolled toward the house.

"Do you want—" she began.

"How about—" he said at the same time.

"What?" she asked.

They might not have much in common, but they were in sync. At least for tonight. His arms around her, he linked his fingers at the small of her back. "I was wondering if you'd come to my room with me."

She grinned. "I was going to suggest mine. It's bigger."

They joined hands and continued their walk. As they reached the kitchen door, he realized something wasn't right.

Given the events of the night before, he listened for any odd sound, a sudden movement from the bushes. Was it possible someone from the outside had broken in? To arrange his liaison with Victoria, he'd asked Mrs. K to change the security code temporarily. She was planning to change the code back again in the morning.

What if somebody had asked her the same thing last night?

No, she would have told them. She feared being blamed for the theft.

Which brought him back to the same question about an "inside job." How else…

The lightbulb finally illuminating, he turned to Victoria. "How do you know how big my room is? You measured when you searched?"

Her eyes danced with mischief. "Mrs. K got me the estate blueprints, and I found something really interesting. Wanna see what?"

11

"Is THIS WHY YOU WERE LATE coming to the cocktail hour?" Jared asked.

Victoria nodded as she brought up the blueprints on her laptop screen. "It was."

He sat beside her on the sofa, the heat from his body enticing. Given the intense satisfaction he'd already bestowed on her, she found the sensation comforting. And promising.

"Your room *is* bigger," he said, glancing around.

"I imagine Rose didn't figure you'd be in yours very long."

"I can do with less."

Victoria studied Jared. No bitterness. Simply stating a fact. So unlike Richard, but the picture she'd had of her potential client as a slightly vain and boastful, but enormously successful and well-connected executive, had changed since she'd arrived.

And not for the better.

She pointed at the screen. "So here's your room."

"Geez. What happened to the blue paper and little white lines?"

The 3-D view of the house and surrounding property resembled a simulated video game, where the viewer could get broad, overhead views or zoom into a room or hallway as if walking through them in real life.

"Rose's interior decorator has a talented technical department."

"No kidding." Jared pointed at the nightstand in his room. "That lamp is sitting exactly there, right now."

Victoria clicked on the lamp. "Designer Thomas Cambridge, circa 1928."

"The woman's obsessed with that time period. Now, what's so interesting?"

Victoria zoomed downstairs to Richard's office, where the bookcases behind his desk clearly revealed a space beyond.

"A secret room?" Jared asked, echoing her thoughts.

"I think we should go snoop."

"I think we should get in bed."

She ran her hand up his chest. "Come on. It'll be fun."

"Hmm. Which would be more fun, sneaking around Richard's office in the middle of the night or getting naked and orgasmic in the middle of the night?"

"So maybe it won't be that entertaining. But the sooner I find this necklace, the sooner we can enjoy the weekend."

"I had a pretty good time tonight."

"Yet here we are…." She indicated the laptop.

Jared said nothing for a second, then sighed. "You honestly think Richard stole his own mother's necklace?"

"Could have. But there's no motivation for him to use his new, high-tech safe in the crime."

"So why are we snooping in this back room?"

"Because he *might* have stolen it. And I'm out of ideas on who else is guilty." Sensing Jared wasn't impressed by that chain of logic, she paused before adding, "There's also the possibility Richard is hiding some embarrassing collection of porn or women's undergarments that I could use to blackmail him into giving me the contract if I don't find the necklace." She couldn't help but smile.

Jared stroked her cheek. "I love how your mind works."

"Come on, let's go."

He pulled her to her feet, and they headed toward the door.

"How are we going to get in the room? Pull out a fake book like in the old mystery movies?"

"We'll figure out something."

Before they reached the door, there was a knock on it. They exchanged a confused look, then Victoria waved him behind her as she opened the door a crack.

"I thought I heard you moving around in here," Richard said, standing in the hall, wearing plaid pajamas and a matching housecoat.

"Just about to turn in."

"Any progress on finding the necklace?"

She hoped her guilty intentions weren't stamped on her face. "I've got a couple of ideas, but nothing definite." Jared slid his finger down the center of her back, and she almost squealed. Gripping the door tighter, she cleared her throat. "Don't worry. I'll manage."

"I have complete faith in you. On that subject, given what happened last night, I'm going to engage the motion sensors."

Damn. "You really think that's necessary?"

"No, but Mother says she can't sleep, knowing the house isn't fully secured."

"Oh. We can't have that." So much for Victoria's grand plans for searching his office. Jared poked her in the back. He was clearly pleased about the change of plans and anxious to wrap up her hallway discussion.

"I suppose if the sensors had been on last night," Richard lamented, "the necklace wouldn't have been stolen in the first place."

"True. What a shame."

Jared poked her harder. What the devil was the man about? She was ready to get rid of Richard and enjoy their limited time together, too, but two minutes one way or the other would hardly—

Double damn.

The alarm code.

Mrs. K had changed it for them, and Victoria assumed the code would be necessary to set the motion sensors.

Richard was going to enter the wrong code.

"The sensors will automatically turn off at 6:00 a.m.," he was saying. "Just be sure you don't wander the halls before then."

Her mind was spinning with a way to tell him about the code change, plus the code itself, but she hadn't been paying attention when Jared entered the numbers earlier. Maybe there'd been a three...? "Right," she said to Richard. "No wandering."

"Sleep well. I'll see you in the morning."

Jared's poking became more insistent. "Uh, Richard?" she began. Licking her lips, she blurted, "I took a late walk on the beach, and Mrs. K changed the security code so I could get in the house."

Richard's face was blank. "Oh."

"Please don't be angry with her. I'm sure she assumed that since I was looking into the theft, she could trust me with the code overnight. She was going to change it back in the morning to the one you use."

Richard waved his hand. "It's perfectly fine. It was wise of both of you to make such careful arrangements. What's the temporary code?"

"Hmm...well, I wrote it down, but I'm not sure I remember..."

Suddenly it occurred to her that Jared was giving her the code. One poke, three pokes, then five—maybe six?—one.

"Oh, now I remember. One, three..." During her extended pause, Jared got the message and distinctly poked five times "...five, one."

"Excellent," Richard said. After a quick smile, he added, "It's a good thing I haven't changed the system to a fingerprint pass code like we have at the office." His pleased expression faded quickly. "There's so little crime out here, I honestly didn't think it was necessary."

"Try not to overreact. I'm sure we'll find the necklace."

"You're sure that caterer and the writer can be trusted?"

Victoria ground her teeth before finding the strength to be pleasant. Blame the hired help and conveniently forget it was his safe that had failed in the first place. What a jerk. "I'm sure. Good night."

She pushed the door closed before he could ruin her mood even further. Turning, she found Jared leaning against the wall with a broad grin on his face.

"Darn. No snooping." He seized her hand and headed toward the bedroom. "Guess we have to move on to plan B."

"Don't you think we should lock the door?"

"What for? The motion detector will shriek like a scalded cat if anybody walks down the hall."

"Like the safe was supposed to protect the necklace?"

"Good point." He made a U-turn, locked the door, then darted into the bedroom.

Before she knew it, her dress was again in a crumpled pile on the floor, along with his clothes, and they were in bed. "Are you always this insatiable?" she asked as he rolled on a condom.

"Stamina is a personal ambition."

"Mission accomplished," she groaned when he slid inside her and carnal delight spread through her body.

He moved his hand beneath her, cupping her backside and angling her hips as he drove deeper. Setting a rapid pace, he seemed to be in no mood for an easy slide into desire. No fooling around, no hesitation. With her arousal at a fever pitch all night, it wasn't long before her need had built to a near-perfect peak.

His firm erection rubbed her center like a live wire, sending sparks over her skin, through her veins, to the core of her being. She let out a whimper as her body went rigid just before the pulses began.

Despite being caught up in her own euphoria, she shared his cry as he followed her into completion.

His heaving chest pressed her into the mattress as his movements subsided, and she clutched him to her, holding his heated body while their breathing fought to recover.

"I'm crushing you," he said a bit later, rolling off with a satisfied groan.

Actually, she'd enjoyed his weight, though she frowned even as the thought occurred to her. After sex, she usually felt the need for space, emotionally as well as physically.

Jared was different from past liaisons in so many ways. Her parents were always formal with each other, never getting overly emotional. It was only when she'd gotten to know Shelby and Calla that she'd become comfortable with spontaneous hugging.

And yet their lives were incompatible. She was a city girl, he was country guy. She shopped for designer shoes, he taught people to ski and dive. She longed for a corner office, he needed wide-open spaces.

He was comfortable with his success, and she was sure she'd never be successful enough.

Lying on his back, he pulled her close. She stroked her hand across his firm chest muscles, the sprinkling of dark hairs tickling her fingers.

Her physical senses were content, her mental ones restless. And the unsettling wave washing over her was only complicating things for her. Did they have anything to talk about besides that stupid, freakin' necklace?

"Earlier, you mentioned you grew up ranching," she said, hoping she didn't sound as if she was reaching desperately for normal conversation. "What kind?"

"Cattle mostly."

She lifted her head. "So you're a real live cowboy, not just playing one on these adventures."

He tipped an imaginary Stetson. "Yes, ma'am."

Impressive, especially since he was naked. "So you're from somewhere out West, I guess."

"Montana. It's still home, though I'm not there much anymore. I bet you were raised in the city."

"New York, *the* city."

"You don't get tired of the noise, the traffic, all those people?"

"No way. Quiet makes me twitchy. Aren't you afraid to live in a place where cows outnumber people?"

"You have a fear of livestock?"

"Not a fear exactly, but after learning that horses—which weigh a good fifteen hundred pounds—have brains the size of a walnut, I'm keeping my distance."

His chest rumbled with his laugh. "But you can pretty much lead them around by the nose with a sugar cube."

"Hmm. Good to know."

"You can't exactly apply the same technique with a speeding taxi."

"No, but waving a twenty-dollar bill works."

"The wild in different forms."

Personally, she thought their preferences seemed hopelessly divergent, even though she had enjoyed the beach and surf yesterday. Beach and surf were outdoorsy, right? Plus, no vast meadows of creepy nothingness, bugs or horses had been involved.

Maybe backgrounds and lifestyles weren't a great topic of conversation, after all.

"Tomorrow I'm going to search everybody's rooms, as well as their luggage," Victoria said briskly. "Last time there was a chance the necklace was misplaced. Now, no stone unturned. Can you keep people occupied while I do?"

"Well, I…*what?*"

She propped herself on her elbow, and he turned to face her. "I'm not really good with pretense and asking sly questions. I'm a direct woman. Time for a new strategy."

"So I've noticed." He slid his hand over her thigh. "But you're being devious by searching without telling people what you're doing."

"Only because I don't want Richard to know what I'm doing, since I'm going to search his secret room, too."

Jared's hand stopped midstroke. "I don't think that's a good idea."

"Why not? You trust him less than I do."

"But if you get caught searching that room, your big contract will be horse dung."

"I have to do something. I'm a PR executive full-time, Robin Hood is only temporary."

Though at least she'd been a willing participant in that project.

She'd been strong-armed this time. But since Coleman Sr. had already emailed her three times since she'd arrived, she assumed he was doing the same with Peter. Rutherford Securities was a big client for their agency, so doing whatever it took to keep Richard happy was vital.

"Search the luggage if you want," Jared said, "but wait for me to help you with Richard's office. You at least need a lookout."

"If the house is deserted, what do I need a lookout for?"

He rubbed his lips against hers. "Maybe I just want to be near you."

She wrapped her arms around his neck, her bare body nestled alongside his. "Maybe?"

His lips grazed her throat. "Definitely."

"Your assistance has been invaluable so far."

"I've always had a knack for critical chores."

She stiffened with insult. "Chores?"

"A term used on the ranch," he said easily. "Here, so close to the city and away from a concentrated gathering of a bovine population, I'd call my skill in certain areas a mission." He slid his fingers down her thigh. "A calling."

The itch spreading through her body made everything else fade away. It didn't matter that they were incompatible, or temporary or anything else that wasn't right. "You realize we're stuck with each other for the night," she whispered.

He kissed her jaw. "Those damn motion sensors."

She arched into his touch. Other than their labored breathing, the house was quiet. For once, she appreciated the silence.

New York Tattletale
A Big Sparkler
by Peeps Galloway, Gossipmonger (and proud of it!)
Hola, City Dwellers!

By the time you've engrossed yourself in my compelling prose, I'll be in sunny Mexico, submersed in a passion fruit margarita—or three—soaking up rays and balmy ocean breezes and wishing you were here to share in my nirvana.

But when I got such a hot tidbit, I naturally had to share it with my rabid readers. (Bless you all.) Thanks to my assistant's loyalty (and the fact that I have a popularity quotient that, frankly, keeps this publication in the black), I'm able to bring you yet another update from the Rutherford estate.

I have to say after the recently thorough performance of my snooper network, I was a bit miffed to hear this latest news, as it's *two and a half days old!*

For shame, right?

Anyway, this bite is much bigger than a tidbit—in fact, it's 99 whopping carats. Yes, it seems Rose Rutherford's latest sparkler is a diamond-and-sapphire necklace, with the big blue rock weighing in almost in triple digits.

Too much, you say?

I do, and often, when referring to the fiery-haired widow, but when it comes to hot gems, I say the bigger, the better.

The central stone necklace, mined in Sri Lanka in the 1920s, is reportedly a stunner, and caused quite a stir at dinner on Thursday night. (Yes, I know, two and half days ago.) But would your zealous correspondent let that get her down?

No way, *amigos!*

Because the real scoop is that at the grand party tonight, the necklace is apparently not part of the dress code.

The wardrobe is, however, full of costumes from the roaring twenties, which will be worn by the fortunate few bunking in the house. The priceless bauble, on the other hand, has been given the night off.

Curious, no?

I'm truly sorrowful if you're stuck in the sticky heat that is Manhattan at the dawn of September, but don't worry, busy bees, I'll drink an extra margarita in honor of your misery and tip my masseuse according to my state of bliss.

Wait. Strike that.

You have my sublime column to make your day—and possibly your entire weekend—so you're undoubtedly content as a cat with a bowl of cream.

Drink up!

La suya en espíritu, si no el cuerpo (Yours in spirit if not body),

—Peeps

JARED SNEAKED OUT OF Victoria's room a few minutes after six Sunday morning.

He took a long, hot shower to try to wake himself up. He hadn't gotten much sleep, but oh, what an excellent way to lose it.

Surely Mrs. K would give him a double shot of coffee once the kitchen was open for business.

Thinking ahead, he decided to be proactive and put on his trunks and a T-shirt. Knowing he'd be in the water all day, he didn't even bother with shoes.

When he got to the dining room, a large poster sitting on an easel dominated the entrance.

A Night of 1920s Culinary Delights
Bathtub Gin
Caesar Salad
Stuffed Clams
Chicken in Wine Sauce
Asparagus Tips au Gratin
Pineapple Upside-down Cake

Victoria arrived behind him as he was reading.

In contrast to his bleak-eyed appearance, she looked refreshed, composed and beautiful as always in a pale green sundress.

He fought to come up with a neutral topic of conversation, and the giant poster seemed a convenient, glaring recommendation.

"How'd she get a printed menu so fast?" he asked, still finding it hard to believe Rose was determined to add a costume party to this already bizarre weekend.

"Shelby's always been a full-service caterer. And Calla's handy on the computer."

Jared studied the elaborate script and color graphics of the featured dishes. "Wasn't Prohibition going on during the twenties?"

"If there's no alcohol, I'm boycotting."

"I'll open a speakeasy in the parlor," he assured her.

"Oh, Jared," Rose began excitedly as she approached. "I'm so glad you're here. I've got great news."

"More?" he queried, fighting to keep the sarcasm out of his tone.

Her eyes danced with fun. "This news is special for you."

Jared didn't have to look at Victoria to know she was smirking. "Can't wait to hear it."

"I found a costume in your size."

Oh, boy. "No kidding."

Rose wrapped her arm around his and led him to the other side of the dining room, where a rolling clothing rack filled with various outfits had been parked. She pulled out a black suit on a hanger and handed it to him.

The pants had white pinstripes, the shirt was black and the tie white. There was a matching fedora. Terrific. He'd be the best dressed gangster at the party.

"And here's yours, Victoria," Rose said, handing her a stop-sign-red satin gown. "You're so tall and thin, you'll look stunning."

Victoria held the dress against her body. "If I don't breathe."

In his effort to picture Victoria in the clinging fabric, Jared nearly forgot his dread at being trussed up like Al Capone.

"Good morning, Calla," Rose said, heading off. "Come see your costume."

"At least you didn't wind up with the tweed suit," Victoria whispered to Jared.

He turned his attention to the costume she pointed to, which was made of gray wool. Yikes. It was due to get up to ninety-seven degrees by afternoon.

"You couldn't force me into that at gunpoint." Smiling, he slid his finger down her dress. "At least there'll be high points to this party."

"Easy for you to say. Everybody there won't be able to count *your* ribs." She regarded the gown at length. "I should probably skip breakfast."

After returning their costumes to the rack, he led her to the buffet, where several chafing dishes had been set up. "But think of all the calories you burned last night."

"And will repeat tonight?" she asked quietly.

"I'm up for it if you are." He placed a spoonful of scrambled eggs on her plate. "You should load up on protein."

"Considering your stamina, I'm gonna need more than one helping."

"You can have all you want."

Her gaze moved to his. "Of you or the eggs?"

"Bo—"

"Did you see my costume?" Peter interrupted. "Very smart. I've always wanted a tweed suit."

Jared covered a laugh with a cough.

"How'd you sleep, Peter?" Victoria asked.

"Like a baby. Probably because of all the skiing." He smiled at Jared. "I haven't been in the water that much since my college swim team days."

Jared nodded even though he doubted Peter had been considered for a swim team since he'd graduated from the tadpole group at his local YMCA.

Peter continued, "Emily said she was restless because of that business the night before. She seemed to think we'd be the next victims." He lowered his voice. "Personally, I think Rose took the necklace herself."

At that wild statement, Victoria looked interested. "Really? Why?"

"She certainly enjoys the spotlight and everyone making a fuss over her."

The irony of this being said by a man who spent every waking moment bragging about imaginary accomplishments was obviously lost on him.

"Even buying the necklace in the first place. Who'd want something with such a sad and gruesome past?" Peter shook his head ruefully. "My Emily would never touch such a thing."

"Rose seemed pretty upset about the necklace being gone," Jared said.

Peter angled his head, looking troubled. "I guess so, but who else would take it? I mean, none of us are thieves."

"How do you know?" Victoria challenged.

Her rival silently considered her question, then raised his finger to make his point. "I did once steal a pen from the office, then lost it on the subway. I felt so guilty I bought an entire box as a replacement. I always wondered how the office manager accounted for the extras in the inventory reconciliation."

Good grief, the man really was a dweeb.

Either out of questions or bored, Victoria shrugged and headed to the table with her breakfast plate.

Jared followed her. As they sat beside each other, she slid her bare foot over his. She'd been wearing sandals, so this wasn't an accidental brush. It took very little to turn him on where she was concerned, but skin-against-skin was a huge enticement.

He remembered her long, sleek legs tangled with his throughout the night. Her glossy hair teasing his skin as she kissed her way across his chest. The glorious sensation of her body contracting around him.

"This house gives me the creeps," Emily said as she settled into the chair on the other side of him.

And the fantasy vanishes....

Within a few minutes, everyone else had joined them at the table. Conversation centered around the activities for the day and, once Rose had left the room to change into her swim gear, a complaint from Emily about her costume being too plain next to Calla's flapper outfit. David also wasn't thrilled with wearing used clothing.

Shelby and Mrs. Keegan wandered around with fresh refills of coffee and juice. When Shelby reached Victoria, she raised her eyebrows. Victoria, in turn, gave her friend a discreet thumbs-up.

A woman's version of a good score was clearly the same as a guy's.

Interesting.

"Could I get some tea?" Emily asked Shelby when she offered to refill her coffee cup.

Her hands full and a sheen of sweat on her face, Shelby nonetheless agreed.

Victoria rose. "I'll get it."

"Thanks," Shelby said. "There should be some in the pantry."

Jared tossed his napkin on the table. "I'll help you."

Victoria gave him a look that clearly said she knew his generosity was tied to getting her alone in the kitchen.

He grabbed her from behind the second they were out of sight, and placed a kiss on her shoulder. "Mornin'."

She squeezed his hands, then wriggled from his grasp.

"You okay?" he asked as she darted into the pantry.

"I'm fine. Let me get the tea, then we'll talk."

He wasn't sure why, but he was suddenly on edge. Had one night been enough for her? Was he not even worthy of the entire weekend? "You weren't running from my touch last night."

She glanced at him over her shoulder, her eyes narrowed. "And I'm not now." She returned to her pantry search. "You're making too much of—" She stopped abruptly. "Oh, my."

She turned around, holding not a box of tea but a black velvet case. The kind you kept jewelry in.

"Rose's?"

"Who else?"

Jared couldn't be sure Victoria was holding her breath as she lifted the lid, but he sure as hell was.

12

THE JEWELRY CASE WAS EMPTY.

Victoria wasn't sure what she'd been expecting. Rose had somehow forgotten she'd tucked her priceless necklace behind her supply of oolong? The thief had freaked out over her comprehensive investigation and decided to dump the booty?

Both scenarios seemed ridiculous, even though she'd dreamed, if only for a second, that this theft ordeal might finally be over.

The simple truth was that she *had* been running from Jared. She hadn't wanted Richard to see them together. She was supposed to be working, making the deal of her career.

Last night had been memorable, but was it worth risking her promotion?

"Do you think that's the case Rose kept the necklace in?" Jared asked.

"Yes. Though we'll have to ask her for verification."

"How did it get in the pantry?"

"No idea." Though her mind raced with possibilities. Why had the case been hidden? To make for easier transport of the necklace? To avoid detection? To make somebody else look guilty?

"Mrs. Keegan isn't the thief."

Victoria blinked, focusing on Jared instead of the case. "I don't think so, either, but I'm going to have to talk to her."

"Finding the empty case in the pantry is an obvious attempt to throw suspicion on Mrs. K. Too obvious, in fact."

"Or Shelby."

Jared shook his head. "After yesterday everybody knows you're looking into the theft. They know you and Shelby are friends. This is intended to point to Mrs. K." His lips twisted in a mocking smile. "What better patsy than the hired help?"

Like him.

She really didn't want to go down that road just now. Their differences were already glaringly obvious. "Maybe we're giving the thief too much credit for being clever. Maybe he or she simply dumped the case in a convenient place. Maybe Emily took the necklace."

Jared looked confused. "How'd you get there?"

"She was the one who wanted tea. Maybe this was her way of confessing."

"Or trying to throw you off."

Victoria snapped the case closed. "Mission accomplished."

"What're you gonna do with it?"

"I have no idea." She was way out of her depths—not a familiar feeling unless her mother was present. "Keep it to myself for now."

"I'm sorry if you two are making out in here," Shelby announced as she pushed open the kitchen door, "but I really need that tea."

"So much for exclusivity on big news," Jared mumbled.

Shelby halted on the opposite side of the island. "What's that?"

Silently, Victoria held up the jewelry case.

Her friend's eyes widened. "No way." She grabbed the case and flipped it open. "That would've been too easy, huh? Where'd you find it?"

"The pantry."

Shelby flung her hand in that direction. "Anybody could

have put it in there. People have been in and out of here all morning."

"Victoria thinks we need to question Mrs. K," Jared said.

"What people?" Victoria asked at the same time.

As their voices clashed, she shifted her attention to him. Considering the annoyed look on his face, she couldn't help but wonder what had happened to the slow, sexy voice whispering, "Mornin'." The justice business was hell on relationships.

Is it? You said you were only having a fling....

Now she was in a relationship? That'd happened fast.

"I'm questioning everybody," she reminded Jared.

"Naturally." He crossed his arms over his chest. "We can't let feelings get in the way of a thorough investigation."

"You two can argue later." Shelby tapped her fingers on the counter. "I've got chicken to marinate. Peter came in earlier, asking for flavored cream for his coffee. Calla offered to help carry the serving dishes to the dining room. Rose wanted me to be sure to set out the blackberry jam Sal's sister-in-law makes and sells to the local—"

"Emily?" Victoria interrupted. She drew the line at interest in homemade jam.

"She hasn't been in here, as I recall," Shelby answered, "but I wasn't here every minute, either."

"Everybody had access," Jared confirmed.

"Exactly. But about Mrs. K…" Shelby bit her lip. "The thing is…her son has a gambling problem."

Victoria's stomach tightened. "How do you know that?"

"She told me last night. She's terrified Richard's going to blame her for the theft."

"Is the son in debt?" Victoria asked.

Shelby winced. "He hocked her pearl necklace last month. She's trying to get him into counseling. You don't honestly think she's guilty?"

"No, but…" Victoria considered Jared's stony expression. "You have to admit this news complicates things."

"How?" he challenged.

Victoria faced him. "Her son sinking in debt gives Mrs. K a good motive."

His eyes narrowed. "So you're gonna follow Richard's suspicions just so you won't lose the contract."

"He doesn't know about the jewelry case or the son!" Victoria snapped, exasperated.

The kitchen door swung open, and Shelby tossed the object to Victoria as if it had suddenly turned into a bomb.

Victoria tucked it behind her back just as Emily rushed into the room. "What happened to the tea?"

Shelby crossed the room and retrieved a box, which she handed to Emily. "Sorry. We got busy with the dinner prep."

Emily stared at them. They were all doing absolutely nothing—except looking guilty. "You people are very strange."

"And you thought she was the odd one," Jared commented as the door clicked shut behind her.

Victoria leaned forward, bracing her elbows on the counter. "I'm going to need a nice long stint in Our Lady of Peace when this is all over."

Shelby angled her head. "Our lady of what?"

"The sanitarium-spa-spiritual retreat I'm going to open when this is all over."

When the next person through the door was Richard, she didn't even blink, but simply slid the empty jewelry case into the drawer in front of her. "I'd like to talk to Victoria alone," he said immediately.

"I need to check on breakfast," Shelby said, scooting from the room.

It was like Grand Central Station in the kitchen. And yet Victoria was sure Jared wouldn't be scooting.

"Jared, don't you have equipment to prepare for the guests?" Richard asked pointedly.

He didn't move. "It's all ready to go."

Victoria knew he wasn't wild about Richard, but for him to outright defy the man was curious. Surely Jared needed the business? And Richard was probably petty enough to tell his wealthy neighbors how uncooperative Jared had been.

Did she really want to work for a such petty, self-important individual?

It'll all be worth it when the weekend is over.

Would it? Because then she'd have to work with the man for the rest of her career.

Surely, though, he'd leave mundane tasks like PR campaigns to his managers. He'd only be around to approve—or disapprove, change, revise, possibly transform—all her team's hard work, in the final stages.

It was no wonder corner offices weren't easy to come by.

"It's fine if he stays, Richard. The whole house surely knows by now I'm looking into the theft."

Richard, no doubt regarding Jared as a viable suspect, was wary when he asked, "Any developments?"

"Nothing concrete. Though I imagine my questions yesterday unnerved some people." She specifically recalled David hyperventilating.

Richard seemed unimpressed. "I'm not interested in psyching out the thief. I want that necklace back."

Instead of rolling her eyes—her first instinct—Victoria tried for humor. "Really? You hadn't mentioned that before now."

Based on the thunderous expression on Richard's face, his sense of humor was as underdeveloped as his sense of fair play.

"Don't get worked up," Jared said calmly. "Victoria has everything under control."

"Does she?" Richard raised his eyebrows. "I assume you've been interrogated?"

"Last night, and thoroughly," Jared answered, even as Victoria stepped on his foot to warn him not to give too much away.

Richard's gaze shifted suspiciously between the two of them. "Uh-huh."

Praying her face wasn't turning red with guilt, Victoria moved toward him, sliding her arm through Richard's as she escorted him to the door. "Go have fun on the water today. I've got everything in hand. Rose will have her necklace back by tomorrow."

"You're sure?" he asked. "My company's reputation is on the line."

"Positive." Either that or she was going to wash her hands of the whole business, call the cops—officially this time— then figure out how to face her mother with her humiliating failure. "Leave everything to me."

She all but shoved him out the door.

Alone with her lover, Victoria would rather do just about anything than continue talking about the theft. But neither did she want to talk about last night. Her emotions were too muddled.

"You didn't tell him about the case," he said.

"No. I agree with you. He'll overreact."

"You're not even sure that's the one for the missing necklace. And I wouldn't advise asking Rose, unless you want the whole house to know about your great find. She can't keep a secret for five minutes."

"I'm going to ask Mrs. Keegan. About the case and her gambling son."

"Victoria, she didn't—"

Victoria held up her hand to stall his argument. "It has to be done."

"Why are you so sure she's guilty?"

"Why are you so sure she's innocent?"

"Instinct. That sweet lady wouldn't steal—even for her son."

Victoria was pretty sure Richard was going to need more than instinct to be convinced. But she didn't want to fight with Jared over details.

"So if you found out my brother had a gambling problem, you'd question me?" he asked.

"Does he?"

Anger flooded his face. "Richard certainly picked the right investigator."

She crossed to Jared. "If you're going to do something, you ought to do it well."

"More advice from Mama."

"Yes, actually." Victoria kissed him lightly. "Don't worry. I'm not going to interrogate Mrs. K under hot lights. Just ask her a couple of straight questions. Meanwhile, you keep an eye on my suspects. Also, if you could chat up Sal, I'd really appreciate it. Nobody can be as easygoing as he seems. Shelby actually thinks he's some kind of crook, but I'm wondering if he's broke and trying to get to Rose for her money."

A smile teased the corners of Jared's mouth. "You've got that all wrapped up in a neat bow, don't you?"

"Come on, finding the necklace will be good for both of us."

He wrapped his arms around her. "You're getting a lucrative client and a corner office. What do I get?"

"I can come up with a suitable reward."

"How 'bout a badge?"

She kissed the underside of his jaw. "The reward I was considering doesn't involve wearing anything at all. Though I'd be happy to draw a star on your chest."

"That's a good deal." He stroked her hair back from her face. "But we're calling the police if we don't find the necklace by tomorrow, right?"

She didn't think telling him that she and her buddies had already called the cops would be wise. Detective Antonio probably wouldn't make official notes about his background checks. Or want anyone to know they'd dragged him into their adventures again. Or even acknowledge he knew them.

"After the barbecue, I'll make the call myself," she promised.

They sealed the pledge with a kiss, one Victoria clung to

not because she wanted assurances of Jared's cooperation, but because she needed his touch.

She didn't need people.

At least not often.

But she needed him. She was crazy about his voice and laugh, his body, the unspoken communication they often shared, even the way he comforted Rose and defended Mrs. Keegan.

And their lives weren't remotely alike.

They didn't want the same things. They didn't even live in the same city. Actually, she had no idea where he lived. Probably in a trailer in the middle of an isolated forest.

She broke the kiss and found the familiar sight of his handsome face inches from her own.

Already familiar. Yet she knew nothing about him.

"Where do you live?" she asked abruptly.

"Officially, in an apartment in the city."

Her jaw dropped. "Manhattan?"

"I'm not there much."

Seeing him in a whole different light, she stepped back. "I thought you were a cowboy."

"I am." Clearly frustrated, he tunneled his hand through his hair. "The adventure company is based in New York and air travel is easy from the city. I'm really never there."

A fact that most likely wouldn't change simply because *she* was there. She was making way too much out of one night. After the weekend, he'd be off to his next job, and she'd go back to hers.

"Makes sense," she said. "Though I can't really picture you in the city."

He slid his hand across her cheek. "I can't picture you out of it."

The goodbye was inevitable. They both knew it. They needed to enjoy each other while they could.

He seemed to come to the same conclusion. "You should start searching and questioning."

"And you need to get out of this house. Go have underwater fun."

He slid his arms around her waist. "With you?"

"I'll be along eventually."

DANGLING HIS FEET IN THE water at the boat's stern, Jared leaned back as he watched his charges bob in the surf on inner tubes.

For the last few hours, they'd loved being pulled behind the boat and jumping the waves. But with the contents of the lunch cooler Shelby had prepared now consumed, they seemed content to float.

He longed for activity. The quiet made him think.

After his night with Victoria, he felt both connected to her and farther away than ever. The relationship couldn't go anywhere, even if he had the necessary time to devote to one. Their lifestyles were incompatible. He'd known that from the beginning. But the reality of separating from her tomorrow was much worse than he'd anticipated.

Then there was that cursed necklace.

The way she was handling the theft was smart and resourceful, and yet he could see her skirting close to the line where her goals were more important than anything else. While he agreed she had to talk to Mrs. K about her son, he didn't like the thought of the housekeeper being embarrassed and under suspicion.

Oh, yeah, 'cause you'd never ignore your conscience to get something you wanted, would you?

He'd purposely kept his financial status from Victoria so he could be the regular guy she needed. The deception also assured she was attracted to him, not his bank account. And since his plan had worked, his lie was worse than anything she had dreamed up. His was premeditated, to his direct benefit.

He needed to leap from his high horse, and remember that Victoria hadn't asked for this responsibility. It wasn't as if she was getting a kick out of pawing through other people's suitcases or asking personal questions. Plus, if she found the necklace, they'd all be better off. He'd be happy to spend the rest of their time together having fun that included a lot of sex and no detective work.

Maybe that's why he felt so lousy and unsettled. The theft had pushed moral buttons he didn't want to face. That supposed jealousy curse had to be the reason he was so possessive of Victoria, resenting Richard anytime he came within ten feet of her. That was why Jared dreaded their parting. He couldn't possibly have lasting feelings toward her.

His attention drawn to Sal as he swam toward the ladder, Jared shook off his worries. Extending his hand, he helped the elderly man onto the boat.

"Thanks," he said, snagging a towel and wiping his face.

Yesterday, Jared had been so distracted by Victoria in her yellow bikini that he hadn't paid much attention to Rose's gentleman friend. But today he'd noticed Sal had the physicality of a much younger man.

Jared could only hope he'd retain as much of his physique at sixty-two.

Obviously, being a crook of some kind kept a guy in shape.

With Victoria doing her part to solve the case, Jared supposed he'd better get moving on his.

He plopped down next to the other man on one of the benches. "So, Sal, how's the jewelry business?"

"Decent, though I'm retired and don't spend much time at the stores anymore. My two sons run the business now, heaven help them. If they keep fighting over everything, they'll never save for a place out here." He stared at the choppy waters around them. "You work all your life for your kids, try to teach them right, then one day you wake up and realize they weren't listening to a damn word."

"I'm sorry about your family troubles, sir. Maybe your sons would be happier with only one of them in charge. Not all kids are alike."

Amusement flickered across Sal's face. "You got kids?"

"No, I am one. My brother runs our family business." He swept his hand across the boat. "I get this."

"How'd you decide who was in charge?"

"A poker game." Jared grinned. "I let him win."

"Because you didn't want the responsibility?"

"Because I knew he wanted it."

"A compromise would be nice. I appreciate you lifting my spirits. One of my dealers found Rose's necklace, you see. I spent weeks searching for just the right birthday gift for her." His eyes turned bleak. "I can't believe it's gone."

How had they missed this? And what, exactly, did it mean? "*You* gave her the necklace?"

He nodded. "I want to marry her, and I was hoping the right gesture would show her how much I love and understand her. We've been widowed long enough. My wife died slowly of cancer, and Rose's husband... Well, I expect you've heard the story. We deserve a little happiness."

So much for the theory that he was using Rose to get to her money. Any doubt about this man's character was embarrassing. This theft was turning them all against each other. "Yes, sir, I agree."

Sal's face flushed. "Sorry to bend your ear about my problems."

"It's fine."

In a flash, Jared realized he'd eliminated not one, but two suspects. Sal wouldn't steal the necklace he'd given to Rose to prove his feelings, and Rose wouldn't use the gift to play drama queen.

Jared wasn't sure who that left as the thief. Though he had a feeling that when they found the necklace, Sal and Rose would break the history of jealousy and betrayal the gems represented, replacing it with something much more powerful and long-lasting.

Love.

"I'M SORRY ABOUT ALL THIS, Mrs. Keegan," Victoria said, handing the housekeeper another tissue. "Can you get your son into counseling?"

"I tried last year." Tears streaked down her pale, powdered cheeks. "He won't admit he has a problem, even though he owes money to people all over the city. Any day I expect the hospital to call to tell me he's been admitted with two broken legs."

Did the mob still do that kind of thing, or had Mrs. K seen one too many TV shows? "I'm sure it won't come to that," Victoria said feebly. She *was* useless with crying women. Where was Jared when she needed him?

"No matter the trouble he's in, I wouldn't take Miss Rose's necklace."

"I believe you." Since Mrs. K had, in fact, burst into tears the instant Victoria had shown her the jewelry case, she doubted the woman had the nerve to squeeze fruit at the farmer's market. "I appreciate you confirming this is the case for the missing necklace. I'd rather not show it to Rose and upset her unnecessarily."

Sniffling, Mrs. K nodded.

You don't seem to have a problem upsetting the hired help, though, do you?

Victoria could practically hear the disappointment in Jared's voice.

She hated upsetting the housekeeper, she really did, but she had to solve the theft and end this. For everybody's sake.

"Why don't you go lie down awhile?" Victoria suggested. Maybe Mrs. K deserved a retreat at Our Lady of Peace.

"No." Her gaze distant, the woman lifted her wobbly chin. "I'd rather get back to work, if you don't mind."

Terrific. She'd ruined this relationship, temporary as it was.

"Sure. Go ahead." *I have that secret room and several guest rooms to search.* "Thanks for your candor," Victoria added as she left the kitchen.

"Oh, V, there you are," Calla said, walking toward her as she headed down the hall. "Why aren't you out on the water with us?"

Where a half-naked Jared was gamboling about. Furious

with herself and the whole damn situation, Victoria made an effort to get ahold of her shame. She'd been given a task. In the spirit of justice, she had a duty to perform. She was going to see it through.

"I have a necklace to find," she said to Calla, scooting around her friend.

"Where are you going?" Calla asked, hot on her heels.

"To the guest rooms. And I'm not just casually looking under the beds and around the doors this time. Can you pick a suitcase lock?"

"No, and neither can you."

"Maybe I shouldn't. But I am."

"Even if you find it, the evidence won't be admissible in court."

Victoria ignored Calla's legal advice and marched up the stairs. "What court? If I find the necklace, I'm putting it on Rose's dressing table."

"What about conspiracy, accessory after the fact?"

"I'm not telling anybody I'm putting it on her dresser."

"But—" Calla jogged up the stairs beside her "—you're going to let a thief get away?"

"If it helps me get my contract, yes." Though she certainly wasn't looking forward to invading her fellow housemates' privacy. The thought of putting her hand in the vicinity of Peter's underwear made her want to gag. Fortunately, Shelby had brought along a healthy supply of disposable rubber gloves— a requirement for every public food service kitchen.

Calla ran around Victoria, stopping her progress. "You're serious."

"Aren't I always?" Seeing her friend's horrified expression, she sighed. Meting out her brand of justice was a heavy burden. Had Robin Hood felt so tormented? "What purpose would it serve by sending this thief to jail?"

"He or she won't steal anything else."

"What if it's Rose?"

Calla looked indecisive. "Uh, well..."

"Or Mrs. Keegan, stealing the necklace because the proceeds will save her son from having his legs broken by the bookies he owes?"

Calla's eyes widened to the size of saucers. "You're not going to search her room, too?"

"Yes, I am." Though only for appearances' sake. Victoria continued up the stairs. "This ridiculousness has gone on long enough. Time for results. I want Richard's contract. I want my promotion. Not to mention I have access to a hot guy who wants to be with me all night long."

At the top of the stairs, Calla planted herself in front of Victoria yet again. "Weren't you with him last night?"

"Yes, which is why I want to be with him again. Get out of my way."

"Fine," Calla said grudgingly, falling into step beside her. "Let's start in Sal's room. I'm beginning to think Shelby's right. He could be a thief."

She had to confess it was an intriguing possibility, but Victoria was hoping for Peter. Talk about wrapping everything up with a neat little bow…

Part of her recognized she was in an annoyed frenzy and not making the most rational decisions. But the rest of her was tired of the pretense. Somebody in the house had that necklace. This wasn't international terrorism or an elaborate crime syndicate. This was simple. And she was out of patience.

Especially for a task that was going beyond, over, under, up and into outer space, given normal professional expectations.

She didn't like the prolonged deceit. In fact, she'd have been great as one of those cops who interrogated people under white-hot lights, like in the old movies. In that smokin' red dress—amid everybody else in black and white—she'd have this case solved in fifteen minutes.

Remembering her costume, she pressed her hand to her stomach. Carrots and celery were going to have to be on the lunch menu.

"You're sure this is the only way?" Calla asked.

She loved her friend truly, but Victoria had to do everything she could to end this mess as soon as possible.

"Pretty sure," she said, focused on the diagram she'd drawn from the computer blueprint program that showed all the rooms that had been assigned for the weekend.

"*Pretty sure* isn't too—"

"Sarcasm, blondie. Get ahold of yourself. In fact, why don't you go take pictures of something?"

Calla lifted the camera clutched in her hand. "I am. I'm recording this entire search process. What if somebody sues you?"

Well, damn. Outside Peter and Emily's door, Victoria halted. Growing up in the Holmes house with a corporate attorney, she'd learned that *sue* was a swear word.

Eyes narrowed, she turned slowly to Calla. "The only way they could sue would be if there was a witness."

Her friend took a step back. "I don't like the look in your eyes right now."

"Have I not effectively communicated how far down the end of my rope I'm currently hanging?"

Calla nodded. "The contract, corner office and great sex with hot guy."

Victoria smiled fiercely. "Exactly."

"Fine. No video." Calla made a show of setting the camera on the floor in the hall. "Like the whereabouts of Sherwood Forest, your secret is safe with me, my lady."

UNFORTUNATELY, EVEN WITH Calla's keen eye, the search proved useless—though Victoria did learn mousy Emily had a fondness for garish purple lingerie. A fact she could have gone a lifetime without knowing.

After all the guest rooms and other bedrooms were examined, Victoria told Calla about the secret place concealed in Richard's office.

As seemed to be the way their luck was going, they found

their host's office locked. *What?* He didn't trust his house-guests?

They even mustered the nerve to ask Mrs. K for a key, which she didn't have. Undeterred, they attempted to pick the lock, without success. If only one of them had been the thief...

Around two, she and Calla wound up in the kitchen, looking for the lunch they'd missed. In the fridge, they found at least twenty pounds of ribs and steaks marinating, presumably for tomorrow's Labor Day barbecue.

"Who's coming to this party?" Victoria wondered aloud. "The Yankees *and* the Knicks?"

"Did you get a look at that dress Rose picked out for you?" Calla asked from behind her. "You can't eat any of this stuff."

Victoria turned and met her friend's gaze. "Thanks, buddy."

"I'm just sayin'." Calla straightened. "That's all for tomorrow, anyway. After this costume party, you can have whatever you want, I guess."

"What I want is that necklace."

"And Jared McKenna."

"Him, too. Oh, look, tuna salad." Victoria removed the plastic dish and slammed it on the kitchen counter.

"You're awfully cranky for a woman whose nights are filled with great sex."

"Night. Singular."

Calla pulled her cell phone from her jeans, checked the screen and sighed as she returned it to her pocket. "One night would suit me."

Victoria ate tuna salad—low-fat mayonnaise—at the kitchen table, while Calla tortured her by relishing leftover veal medallions from last night's dinner.

Licking her fingers, Calla handed Victoria a napkin and took another for herself. "What are you going to wear under that dress tonight?"

"Not a whole hell of a lot." Victoria shoved back her chair. "I think I'll lie by the pool. Wanna come?"

Calla grinned. "Nope. You'll try to drown me."

"How could you possibly know that? I'm the queen of deception."

Rising, her friend patted her cheek. "But I've known you too long to be fooled. Let's head out in the dinghy and join everybody else on the yacht."

"That's a better idea than any I've had all day."

"Don't beat yourself up about it. The grand search is a time-honored tradition in all detective fiction."

"But if it's not anywhere in Rose's room, and not in any of the guestrooms, where—"

"Ooh!" Calla whirled from the table. "Maybe the thief has the necklace with him or her, stuffed down in the bottom of a beach bag."

"That seems risky."

"Swiping the necklace already takes care of that."

"Good point." Honestly, Victoria still had no idea what might have happened to Rose's necklace, who might have taken it, if anybody, and why. The necklace, supposedly cursed by jealousy, was certainly valuable. Not easily pawned, and too recognizable to be worn once the police sank their investigative teeth into this whole messy business.

Her contract was a myth. Shelby wouldn't get any more Southampton bookings after the Rutherfords told the story of the botched search and the tattling to the law. Detective Antonio would resent them forever, which would make Calla miserable.

Where was a band of merry men when you needed them?

Maybe Jared was having better luck.

As the two friends prepared to leave the house, Calla's cell phone rang. "Hi, Devin," she said brightly, after a glance at the screen. "I'm going to put you on speakerphone. Victoria's with me."

"Did you kill anybody yet?" was his first, dry question.

"No," Calla returned. "But Victoria did get a great costume for tonight's big party. You wanna come out and join us?"

"Costume party?" the detective asked.

"Rose's idea of Labor Day fun apparently has a lot in common with Halloween," she explained. "We have plenty of outfits to pick from. I'm sure we can find one for you."

"I'll pass," Antonio said.

"Wise choice," Victoria commented. "Everything's fine out here."

"No, it's not," Calla argued. "We can't find the necklace anywhere."

Victoria jabbed her elbow in her friend's side and frantically shook her head.

"What necklace?" the detective predictably asked.

"Some old thing of Rose's that she's misplaced," Victoria explained quickly, before Calla could blow their secrecy completely. "Nothing to worry about. Did you find out any interesting financial details about the guests?"

Thankfully, Antonio either decided Calla had misspoken or simply didn't care about the necklace. "Like I figured, that palace you're staying in is loaded with rich people. No money motive there. Strike David the PA for that reason, too. He's paid well, but lives modestly. Only ones I can see who might be in a financial pinch are Marion Keegan and the Standish couple."

"We know about Mrs. Keegan's son and his gambling problem," Victoria interjected. "What about the Standishes?"

"They bought a condo in the city last year and can barely make the payments. They also spend a small fortune at a gourmet market on East Fourteenth Street."

"Ha! See, I told you." Heart soaring, Victoria longed to dance around the room, wondering how quickly she could search Peter and Emily's room again. That necklace *had* to be in there. "This is perfect."

Calla looked crestfallen. "You're sure the Rutherford family is wealthy?"

"As King Midas," Antonio answered.

"And what about Sal Colombo's jewelry business?" she

asked. "He's in debt up to his eyeballs, isn't he? Perfect excuse to turn to thievery."

"Sorry, Agent Ness," the detective quipped, as Victoria longed to remind her pal that Shelby was the one who'd come up with the Shifty-Eyed Sal theory. "His chain of stores netted him tons of dough over the years. And there's McKenna, too."

Victoria stared at the phone. "Jared? He works for an adventure tour company, not a jewelry store."

"Yeah, I got that, though he *owns* the tour company. Pretty profitable, actually. Who knew? But his real fortune comes from ranching, jointly held by him, his parents and his brother."

"Real fortune?" Victoria echoed, as her heartbeat picked up speed.

Antonio named a figure that had her eyes popping wide. A figure that would get even her parents' attention.

"That's not possible," Victoria said slowly, as Calla grabbed her hand.

"Problem?" the detective asked.

"No," Calla said, for which Victoria was grateful, since she seemed incapable of opening her mouth. "Thanks so much for your help. And remember you're invited to the barbecue tomorrow if you want to come."

"I'll see if I can clear my calendar."

Calla ended the call, then immediately pulled Victoria into her embrace. "Oh, honey, I'm so sorry."

Victoria's throat had closed, preventing her from speaking. A thief and a liar, and she'd been fooled by both.

13

JARED DOUBLE-CHECKED THE ROPE securing the boat to the dock, then headed directly toward the pool deck. He moved quickly, wondering, as he had for the last several hours, why Victoria hadn't shown up for the afternoon water sports.

Shelby had used her cell phone to call Calla, who'd said she'd decided to take pictures instead of coming out, and that Victoria wanted to lie by the pool. Since Victoria didn't sunbathe, he could only conclude she'd chosen solitude over being with him.

Maybe she was tired. They hadn't gotten much sleep last night.

And yet he couldn't imagine simple exhaustion had kept her from chatting up Richard. Peter had certainly taken advantage of her absence.

His pulse hammering unreasonably hard, he stalked up the pathway, resisting the urge to break into a run when he saw her long, slender body barely covered by a purple bikini as she stretched out on one of the shaded loungers.

"Hi," he said, perching on the edge of the chair. "We missed you this afternoon."

"I needed some time alone," she said.

With her sunglasses hiding her eyes, he couldn't gauge her mood. He gave her a weak smile. "I could have used your help keeping Peter from boring everybody with his story about catching a shark while deep-sea fishing last year."

"I'll bet."

"I guess you didn't find the necklace in your search."

"No."

Something was clearly off with her. Awkwardly, he cleared his throat. "I did pretty good with Sal." He recounted his conversation with the former jewelry store owner. "So that's Rose and Sal off the suspect list."

"How do you figure?"

"They wouldn't hurt each other that way. That necklace is a symbol of their love."

"A necklace that literally caused a murder? How romantic."

That's it. He was done tiptoeing around her mood. "What's with you?"

"I guess I'm a bit more skeptical than you," she said, shoving her sunglasses to the top of her head, enabling him to see the fury in her eyes. "Maybe Sal bought that necklace to buy Rose's love. Maybe he stole it. Maybe he wrapped it up with a pretty bow, but when Rose didn't return his feelings, he decided to take it back. Maybe he *lied*."

The frigid, angry woman before him was a stranger. "Sal didn't steal the necklace," Jared stated.

She rose, thrusting her arms into the sleeves of a robe that had been lying over the back of her chair. "I think you're partly right. We can eliminate them—at least if the motive was money. Both of them are, in fact, very wealthy."

"I could have told you that."

"Yes, I bet you could. Since your bank account is ranked right up there with theirs. Apartment in the city, huh?"

Dread crawled through Jared's body. Victoria's coldness, her distance, her absence that afternoon…it all finally made sense. *She knows.* "How'd you find out?"

"A police detective friend of Calla's agreed to do a financial background check on everybody here."

"When did you call the police?"

"Yesterday. I'm not a fool, Jared. I knew we needed help. I tried to do it discreetly."

"And you asked the cops to check on me?"

She narrowed her eyes. "Don't you dare try to turn this back on me. I never suspected you. Calla asked him to verify everybody's status."

He reached for her hand. "Let me explain."

She jerked away. "You've got a lot of damn nerve, warning me off about Richard, harping about his lack of trustworthiness, even implying I was compromising my ethics for questioning Mrs. K."

"That's not why I…" He stopped, at a loss on how to explain why he'd lied, especially since the reason now seemed ill-advised at best and selfishly pompous at worst. "It wasn't like that."

"*You* were the one I shouldn't have trusted," she practically spat.

"Victoria, don't go. I—"

Love you, he realized with a jolt as she stormed away.

He loved her.

HER FINGERS WRAPPED AROUND HER mascara wand, Victoria's hand jerked as someone knocked on her door.

Cursing quietly at the black streak marring her cheek, she called, "Come in!"

She dearly hoped it was Shelby with an emergency martini delivery.

It was Richard, already trussed up in his costume and looking like a constipated banker.

As he stood in the doorway between the bedroom and the den area, she resisted the urge to scream. "Sorry to barge in," he said, "but I'd like to talk to you privately for a minute."

After making sure the tie on her robe was secure, she waved her hand toward the outer room and went to sit beside him on the sofa. "What can I do for you?"

"I've become frustrated with your lack of progress on finding my mother's necklace."

Of course you have. "Me, too."

"Perhaps I should have put Peter in charge."

Victoria ground her teeth and said nothing.

"But then he hasn't been eliminated from the suspect list as far as I'm concerned," Richard went on. "Let's face it, he might be a brilliant public relations man but he doesn't have your pedigree."

"If you crossbred him with the right Lhasa apso, you never know."

Richard pursed his lips. "Do you think now is the right time for jokes?"

"Do you think now is the time to call the police?"

When an insulted look washed over his face and he started to rise, she grabbed his arm and held him in place. "Sorry." She let go of him and stood herself, then paced in a circle before facing him. "I can't believe I'm saying this, but I'm beginning to think I'm in over my head with this theft."

"I see."

"The police are better equipped to handle this kind of thing. I'm sure if we explained the need for discretion, they'd support that effort. This is Southampton, for heaven's sake. They're used to citizens who demand privacy."

"I thought I made it clear," Richard said, his voice hard, "that if you don't find the necklace and expose the thief, I'm taking my business elsewhere."

"To Peter."

He shrugged. "Probably not."

"You just called him a brilliant PR man."

"I was being kind."

Victoria tamped down her temper as dread took over. "So you're saying Coleman will lose your business completely?"

"That's a definite possibility."

And that statement made no sense. "Will we or won't we

lose Rutherford Securities as a client if I don't produce the necklace?" she demanded.

"I haven't decided, but you can be assured an unhappy client is not a secure one."

She couldn't believe how fast everything was falling apart. She was regretting this entire weekend more by the second.

Except for Jared…

But she wasn't thinking about him now. Or ever, if she could manage.

"One more thing," Richard said, rising. "I'm not one to normally pry into people's personal lives…."

But let me guess—you're going to, anyway?

"Do you think it's wise to get involved with a man like Jared?" he finished.

He had to be kidding. "Involved?" she echoed.

"I saw you returning from your boat ride last night."

"Did you?"

"Jared's not a bad guy or anything, but he's transient. Always running off to this part of the world or that one. And do you honestly think you could take him to a formal event in the city? He rarely wears shoes."

Despite her own outrage concerning her lover, she wouldn't let Richard put him down that way. "Jared could fit in anywhere he wanted."

"I'm sure you think so." Richard's smile was condescending. "He seems perfectly comfortable charming women into believing anything he wants them to."

She longed to tell him to get lost, but instead bit her tongue. An important Coleman client was on the verge of leaving the agency. Forget her corner office; she could lose her job with this blunder.

"Thank you so much for the advice," she said, forcing fake sweetness into her voice as she escorted him out. "I'll be careful."

Ridiculously, when she pressed her back to the door, tears flooded her eyes.

Why was she devastated over some guy's lies? And she didn't mean Richard. Clients were generally difficult, unreasonable and demanding, and they always acted in their own best interest. At least Richard had the sense to recognize Peter wasn't up to the task of handling the Rutherford Securities contract.

Lovers were different. They were supposed to offer refuge from her fast-paced life. They were supposed to be a release.

And since intimacy was often difficult for her, Victoria liked rules and predictability. Usually, if men were going to be deceitful, they overestimated their power, status or finances. Who downplayed them? Was that noble or nuts?

All she knew right now was that her meticulous plans, her perfect assent to the top of her profession, had been destroyed by a few hunks of rock and an ego the size of…well, those big hunks of rocks.

Not to mention she had a body-hugging red satin dress to wear through an interminably lousy dinner with her ex-lover and her might-never-be-realized client.

She wondered how her mother dealt with lost deals.

Knowing her, The Legend rolled her shoulders and geared up for the next one. The woman didn't make too many mistakes, after all.

Rolling her own shoulders with a confidence that might even impress the renowned Joanne, Victoria headed to the bathroom to finish getting ready.

After carefully dabbing away the black smear Richard had caused with his abrupt knock, she leaned toward the mirror and again picked up her mascara wand.

At yet another tap on her door, causing a fresh black smear on her cheek, she let loose an entire string of curses. Not taking any chances this time, she stalked to the den and opened the door a crack.

And saw a martini glass with two giant speared olives floating in clear liquid.

She flung open the door to find Shelby and Calla behind

the offering of solace. "Bless you," she said, plucking the crystal from Shelby's tray and stepping back to invite her friends inside.

They were already dressed in their costumes. Calla made a great flapper in her silver satin with black fringe. Shelby wore a tarty French maid outfit.

At Victoria's scrutiny, Shelby said, "Rose wanted Mrs. K to wear a matching one, but Mrs. K turned so pale I thought she was going to faint, so I suggested an alternative. She looks like a prison matron, but at least she's covered."

Victoria turned to Calla. Even though her legs were exposed, the top was flouncy around her waist.

"Wanna switch?" Victoria asked her, knowing she probably wouldn't be able to breathe in hers.

"No way." As Calla shook her head, her feathered headband brushed her cheek and her wheat-colored, corkscrew curls framed her face like a porcelain doll. "I may look like I escaped from a Broadway show, but my generous curves would never fit in that red tube Rose gave you to wear."

Victoria sincerely hoped she didn't look as pitiful as she felt. "I don't feel like eating, anyway." After taking a sip of her cocktail, she acknowledged her buddies' sympathetic expressions with a shake of her head. "I'm fine."

"No," Shelby said, wrapping her arm around Victoria's shoulder, "you're not."

They escorted her into the bedroom, where they all plopped at the end of the bed. Nobody said anything. The disappointment Victoria felt was one they'd all dealt with at times over the years. Life in the city could be tough and even cruel. Men were disappointing, jobs often sucked and bosses were unreasonable. Finding a way to survive was a matter of pride.

"You know you have a mascara stain on your cheek," Shelby said finally, dabbing away the smudge with a tissue she grabbed from the dresser.

"Don't be too hard on Jared," Calla said. "Especially since it's sort of my fault he lied."

"How do you figure that?" Victoria asked.

"I told him about the rich, insensitive guys you usually go out with and suggested you needed a regular guy."

Victoria blinked in shock. "So he lied based on your lousy advice?"

Calla's face flushed. "Hey, it wasn't lousy. You were happy as a clam a couple of hours ago."

Maybe, Victoria conceded silently. "And what guy did I date that you found so insensitive?"

"Come on, V," Shelby said. "The last two, the surgeon and the tax attorney? Their egos were off the charts."

"Jerks," Calla asserted.

"Yeah, well…" Victoria fell silent. Jared was worth twenty of either of those two. No use arguing about the facts.

She wanted to hold on to her fury and righteous indignation, she really did. But she knew the apprehension inside her wasn't only because of his deception; it was much, much worse. "I don't want to talk about him."

Shelby slid her hand down Victoria's arm. "But, V—"

"Please. Save it for later." She took a final sip of the chilly martini before rising to set the glass on the desk. She needed now more than ever to be clearheaded. Facing her friends, she told them the one thing they could help her fix. "We have to find that necklace or Coleman's going to lose the Rutherford contract completely."

Her friends exchanged a look, not surprised, but resigned.

"That Richard is a piece of work," Shelby said.

"Yeah." Given that he'd invited her nemesis to challenge her, she'd known Richard's loyalty wasn't something to count on. But she had to admit, she hadn't seen his absolute desertion coming. No doubt because she was more focused on Jared than her job. "Any sleuthing ideas we haven't already tried?"

"We can still follow up with Peter and Emily on their debt," Shelby said encouragingly.

"True." The idea gave Victoria a spark of hope.

"Are you sure you want to do this at all?" Calla asked

frankly. "You once talked about opening your own agency, having a small, focused client list. Why settle for playing Richard's fall girl?"

Victoria cast a sideways glance at Shelby. "I recall saying that after a lot of pizza, wine, ice cream and too many chick flick DVDs."

"That doesn't mean it isn't a good idea," Shelby said.

"I'm supposed to follow my mother's success," Victoria reminded them, and herself, albeit reluctantly.

Calla surged to her feet. "Supposed to is crap. You don't need to follow her path. Make your own."

The notion had crossed Victoria's mind many times, but she'd always been too proud to be labeled a quitter. Or marked as too scared to live up to The Legend.

"I've always wanted to do more with charities." Victoria shrugged, though she felt anything but casual. "But Coleman has always kept the philanthropic budget strict, and he didn't want his best directors on the write-off stuff."

"It's not like you need the money," Calla reminded her.

"Starting a PR business is a lot of work," Victoria argued.

Calla raised her eyebrows. "You're afraid of hard work now?"

"It's not about working hard, it's working smart," Victoria said. "Coleman has an impeccable reputation they've been building for more than sixty years. You don't jump into this market with a one-woman show and expect to compete with that caliber of a company."

"So don't compete, be unique," Shelby said, then grinned.

"Boy," Victoria said drily, "I can't wait to put that on a business card." Considering the bleak state of her career, she added, "As I'm in imminent danger of losing my job, we'll likely broach this subject again soon. So feel free to hold on to your proposals until then."

Her friends exchanged a worried glance. "You're not going to lose it, are you?" Calla asked.

Victoria forced a fake smile. "Who knows? The night's young."

Shelby guided her toward the closet. "Let's get you in that dress. You never know, if the thief's one of the guys, he might confess the second he sees you."

She doubted that would happen, but she was looking forward to seeing Jared's reaction. If he hadn't turned out to be a big fat fibber, he could have been the one to help her out of the dress later. As a vision of that fantasy wavered before her, desire slid through her belly.

Who was she kidding? She'd probably take one look into those melted-chocolate-brown eyes and throw herself in his arms.

After stepping into the fluid length of red satin, she sucked in her belly as tight as it would go while Calla inched up the zipper. In the mirror, Victoria surveyed her black hair, matching swoop of cat-eye black liner and bright red lips. She might feel lousy, but she at least looked the part of a 1920s vamp.

"Wowee," Shelby said. "You can be the bad cop when we interrogate. Jazz Hands over there can be good cop."

Calla swept her hand down her ensemble. "I like it. I'm wearing it the next time we go out to a club."

Victoria slid on a pair of silver heels. "Let's get on with this."

Maybe Jared would throw himself at her feet.

On the way down the hall, she silently conceded that she'd overreacted to his lie, particularly as Calla had given him the idea. They'd met two days ago. Why did she have the right to know his personal financial information? Why did it matter that he hadn't admitted he owned the company he worked for? The fact that he'd called out Richard for his lack of ethics might be treading the line of hypocritical, but that didn't make him less accurate.

Besides, the real reason she was so angry was because Jared was getting too close. Because all she could think about was the fact that they were going their separate ways tomorrow. Her feelings for him were much deeper than she wanted to admit. Was she finding a reason to push him away?

Would her necklace challenge have been easier if she'd kept her distance? No. But would she regret letting him go without one last night together? Definitely.

Their plan to search Richard's concealed room was still pending. She had to somehow get a key to the office. Ruthanne, maybe? The idea of learning the secret contents could swing everything in a new direction.

And if Victoria found something illicit, would she use that knowledge to strong-arm him into giving her the contract?

Yesterday, she wouldn't have hesitated to use any advantage. A few hours ago, during her mad search, she'd still been determined to push and sacrifice.

Now, she wasn't so sure.

As her friends—and Jared—had reminded her, integrity was worth a great deal. Maybe she wasn't destined to be The Legend, Second Generation. Maybe this was her opportunity to find her own success, live as she wanted, not as was expected.

When she reached the top of the stairs, she smoothed her hand over her hair. She'd spent the day fuming and regretting. It was time to make something happen.

AT THE FOOT OF THE STAIRS, Jared paced. He'd reluctantly donned his historical costume, even though he'd never felt less like attending a party in his life.

He had no idea how to fix the mess he'd made of his and Victoria's affair, but he knew he had to try.

It didn't seem possible that he loved her after knowing her for so short a time, but it was true nonetheless. He'd been kind of in love during high school a couple times, then once in college, but never as an adult.

He'd never felt anything like this.

Even though hope of a real relationship seemed as far from his grasp as the necklace was from everybody else.

A movement at the corner of his eye drew his attention. Glancing up, he felt his heart literally stop before zooming into motion again like a rocket taking flight.

As he'd imagined it would, the red satin gown fit Victoria perfectly, the tiny straps exposing her sleek shoulders, while the dress itself glided down her tall, lean body with the rapt attention of a lover's adoring hands.

He wanted to be those hands.

Flanked by her friends, Victoria stopped at the base of the stairs. Her gaze roved over him. "The suit's nice."

"Mrs. K let out the hem in the pants," he said nervously and unnecessarily.

When he looked into Victoria's eyes, every intimate touch, gesture and word that had passed between them flickered through his memory like a movie at triple speed. He shouldn't *try* to fix things between them, he *had* to.

Briefly forgetting how far apart they truly were, he reached for her hand.

She froze him with her icy stare, stepped around him and, elegant as a queen, strolled toward the living room.

"I need to get back to the kitchen and direct the waitstaff Rose hired for the party," Shelby said, making a quick, uncomfortable exit.

Calla raced after her. "I'll help."

Jared was left standing in the hallway like an idiot, with his hand extended toward nothing.

He barely caught the identical and encouraging smiles Shelby and Calla sent him over their shoulders. He was too busy noticing Victoria's gown dipping low in the back, exposing miles of creamy skin, highlighting the bright red bow tied just above her backside.

A cold sweat broke out on his brow.

Additional correction: if he didn't fix the resentment between them, he was going to implode.

By the time he found the strength to head into the living room, Rose and Sal had also descended the staircase. After gaining a new appreciation for the other man, who loved a woman determined to keep him at a distance, Jared briefly kissed Rose's cheek, bowed, then stepped back, allowing the couple to enter the room arm in arm.

When he crossed the threshold, a waiter offered a glass of champagne from his tray. So far, only the weekend guests and residents of the house were present, though the friends and neighbors were due anytime.

Noting that she stood between Peter and Emily, Jared wasn't sure how to get Victoria to himself and not screw up her investigating, which she had to be doing to have purposely sought out that pair.

He strode toward the group, knowing he couldn't stand to the side and wait for her to forgive him, either.

"Hi, Jared," Emily said brightly when he reached them.

He brushed his lips across her cheek. "You look lovely."

She beamed, holding out one side of her dark green skirt. Give Rose credit, she'd found a way to highlight the best of Emily's looks. And that was saying something, with her standing beside Victoria.

"Thank you," she said, her cheeks flushing.

Straightening, he sipped his champagne and found Victoria glaring daggers in his direction.

Because he'd dared come near her, or because he'd kissed Emily?

He smiled and toasted her. She was severely mistaken if she thought he'd been run off by one mistake and a few harsh words. They'd had fun in the last couple of days, but the truly special moments were in front of them.

Or they could be.

"So, hey," he said, his gaze sweeping the group, "that necklace of Rose's is still missing. Anybody know where it might have gotten to?"

Emily blushed; Peter was obviously insulted; Victoria looked homicidal.

Jared shrugged. *Sorry, folks. I've got limited time here.*

We need to move this business along. "No? What a shame. I guess Richard'll have to call the cops if it doesn't turn up by tomorrow."

Peter choked on his champagne.

While Victoria turned the same shade as her dress, Jared patted her colleague on the back. "Guilty conscience, Pete, ole buddy?"

"Of course not," he sputtered. "How dare you—"

Victoria stepped between them. "He's kidding. Too much sun. And sea air. You know how a good breeze can affect a man's judgment."

A breeze? That didn't make any sense, and why was she talking so fast about nothing? Hold on a second…

She jerked Jared toward her with a viselike grip on his wrist. "Could I speak to you privately for a second?" Already leading him away—which was exactly what he'd wanted in the first place—she glanced back at Peter and Emily. "Sorry. See you at dinner."

Dragging him along, Victoria boldly stalked down the hall and into Richard's office. "What do you think you're doing?" she demanded, releasing Jared so suddenly he had to rock back on his boot heels to keep from stumbling.

He quickly checked the room to make sure they were alone. Books, plaster busts and paintings surrounded him. Nothing that breathed, though. How had he gotten her to himself with so little effort?

"You babbled," he blurted.

Her expression could have frozen the fires of hell. "Excuse me?"

"To Peter and Emily. You babbled."

"I did not. Are you out of your mind? What if one of them took the necklace?"

"What if they did? It's about time we rattled this thief's world."

"Maybe so, but I was trying to find out more about their financial problems. Calla's cop buddy says—"

Snagging her champagne glass, he set it on the desk and wrapped his arm around her. "I interrupted. Sorry. I'm sorry for a lot of things. Wanna give me a second chance?"

Though her gaze probed his without the fury from earlier, her body was stiff. "You lied," she reminded him.

"I did. Lousy thing to do."

"Did you do it because of what Calla said?"

He did love her directness. "Partly. I didn't want to be like the guys in your past. Besides, people—women especially—have used me for my money in the past. Surely the same thing has happened to you. I've learned to protect myself."

"So you were protecting yourself from my greedy nature."

"I wanted you to like me," he argued. "I didn't want you to look at me like every other guy you've been with, then quickly dumped." He cupped her jaw. "I want more."

Her perfume, faintly floral and full of elegance, ignited his senses. He was completely at her mercy, he realized. If she pushed him away, his heart was going to snap in two.

"Me, too," she said, her voice low as she slid her hands up his chest. "We have one more night. I don't want to waste it."

"We could have more than that."

"How?" She looked genuinely confused. "You'll be off to the next adventure in a matter of days. When's your next job?"

He winced. "I fly to Acapulco tomorrow night. There's a restaurant at the top of La Quebrada Cliffs. I'm performing in their show for a few days. But I'll be back in the city by the weekend."

"You're going to jump off a cliff? On purpose?"

Certain he wasn't going to impress her when he admitted he was, he nodded anyway. "Dive, actually."

"And after that?"

"I'll stay in New York if you ask me."

She shook her head, regret filling her eyes. "But I won't. How could I?"

This couldn't be impossible. Obviously, she didn't want

him as much as he did her. "But tonight?" he asked, not knowing where else to begin.

"I'm all yours." She pressed her lips to his in what she certainly intended to be a brief touch, but he clutched her against him, angling his head to deepen the kiss.

Euphoria swam through his body, and the promise of even greater pleasures enticed him to move his hands across her bare back and down her silk-clad sides. She moaned, and he gloried in the realization that she wore literally nothing beneath the clinging gown.

He wanted so much more than one night, but for now he'd take what she offered. How could he not?

"And about the necklace…"

He nuzzled her neck, murmuring, "What necklace?"

She paid no attention to his pretense at ignorance. "Unless somebody miraculously confesses to taking it during the party, I'm breaking into…" She shoved him back. "Hell, we're here."

He glanced around at the books and stodgy decor. "Not the most romantic spot, I realize, but it's private, so…" Catching the determined gleam in her eye, he stopped. "You didn't search here earlier?"

She cleared her throat, no doubt remembering he'd made her promise she wouldn't search without backup. "Calla was supposed to be a lookout, but the room was locked, Mrs. K didn't have a key and we couldn't break in."

"Not even with a bobby pin?"

She threw him a disgruntled look. "Not even then."

He spread his arms. "It's wide-open now."

"Exactly." Her gaze darted to the door. "Let's snoop."

"Now? The other guests are due any minute." Even as he said the words, the doorbell rang. "Damn. No way will Richard leave his office open during the party."

"Maybe I can get a key from Ruthanne," Victoria said hopefully.

"If she has one."

The sound of raised voices and laughter echoed down the hall. *Think, McKenna.*

Hey, a key. He fumbled through the desk drawers until he found exactly that. A handy white tag that said Office Spare was attached to the key ring.

When he held it up for Victoria, she braced her hands alongside his cheeks and kissed him. "Brilliant."

They slipped out of the office and back into the parlor. "Shall we synchronize our watches to ten-thirty?" he asked. "The fireworks should be under way by then."

"Sure." She laid her hand on his jacket sleeve. "If I don't find that necklace, I'm probably going to lose my job. Richard's threatening to pull his business from Coleman."

Of course he was.

Knowing how much her job encompassed her whole life, Jared squeezed her hand. "I'm sorry."

"It wouldn't be the end of the world, I guess."

Just the world she'd sacrificed for and worked so hard for. "Somebody else will hire you in a minute, and your mother will get over you not following in her footsteps."

"But will I?"

"Absolutely. You can come work for me. I can always use another cliff diver."

Victoria laughed. "Mother would *never* get over that."

14

At dinner, Victoria chatted with genuine enthusiasm, recognizing that with twenty extra people plus waitstaff in the house, it would be easy for her and Jared to sneak back to Richard's office for the search.

In passing, she managed to tell her friends that she and Jared had made up, so the night ahead was promising in more ways than one.

Then, with him safely out of her system, she could go back to concentrating on her career. While at odds with him all afternoon, she'd been so busy wallowing that she'd let herself anticipate, even dread, failure. How could there be any doubt she was going to find the necklace? When she did, she was going to be busy making plans to redecorate her new office, brainstorming the new safe campaign with her ad team and relishing her mother's praise.

Victoria wouldn't have time to think about a rich cowboy she'd fooled around with for a weekend.

And why did that sound so superficial and empty?

To distract herself from her unsettled feelings, she glanced around the room.

The antique dining table had been moved out, replaced by several smaller ones covered in deep blue cloths and accented with candles and white flowers floating in clear glass centerpieces. Victoria was again impressed with Shelby's ability to throw a party with style and class, as well as excellent food.

The mix of costumes and regular clothes was a little strange, but anybody expecting Rose to be ordinary was doomed to disappointment.

Their hostess was elegant in a sparkling gold sequined gown with ostrich feathers decorating the sleeves. Sitting next to an attentive Sal, she looked radiant.

She didn't appear upset in the least by her missing jewelry. Actually, now that Victoria was paying attention to something other than the steamy stares Jared had been giving her from across the room, she noticed a stunning diamond-and-ruby bracelet encircling Rose's wrist.

How many priceless gems did the woman own?

"That's a beautiful bracelet, Rose," Victoria said as the waiters served the chicken.

When her face lit up, it was obvious she'd been waiting for someone to comment. Which nobody had, since the last time a piece of jewelry had been discussed at dinner, it had disappeared soon after.

"Thank you," she said, lifting her wrist so the diamonds caught the chandelier's light. "It's a gift from Sal."

"David helped pick it out," Sal said modestly. "He has exceptional taste."

Another flashy gift? Score a major point for Sal. He was one determined suitor.

Receiving elaborate gifts from lovers always made Victoria uncomfortable. She could buy her own jewelry, after all, and the implied commitment that came with something as permanent as diamonds wasn't a place she wanted to go with any guy.

Though she had bought a ring that reminded her of Jared's eyes.

As the rest of the table gushed over Rose's present, Victoria's gaze was inexplicably drawn to Jared's. The look on his face was contemplative.

Was he hoping dinner would end soon, so they could begin their search? Was he thinking Rose was crazy for tempting the thief? Or was he wondering if the chicken had come from a free-range farm?

Hold on. A new temptation for the thief. Why hadn't she thought of that?

If Rose locked this valuable in the safe, and it went missing during the night...

Then they'd have to call the police, and Victoria's contract hopes would disappear just as rapidly and bizarrely as the jewelry had.

However, if she could catch the thief in the act...

So in between hot kisses, you're going to peek into the hall to see what's what?

This was why she didn't mix business and romance. Emotional questions that battled against time commitments were more complicated than any media strategy.

Shelby stopped by as the dessert plates were being cleared. "Enjoy that hunky man instead of obsessing about the missing necklace and the crappy construction of Richard's precious safe."

"Later."

"We're serving after-dinner drinks on the porch during the fireworks."

Victoria glanced at her watch. Ten-twenty. Perfect. "Cover for us."

"Will do," Shelby whispered as she moved to the next table.

When the first shower of sparks rained over the backyard, Victoria ducked into the house and headed for Richard's office. As she stepped out of her shoes and crept around the room, lit only by the moon's glow through the window, she wondered if she really was in a historical time warp.

She paused, considering the lack of significance this party, the jewels and fireworks must have in the grand scheme of things. Even her ambitions failed in comparison.

And that was saying something.

Still, her life was on hold, waiting for the next act. And the beauty of celestial bodies wasn't going to change anything. She needed to get through this weekend, find that necklace and save Richard's reputation.

By the time Jared slipped into the office, she was already knocking on the bookcases behind Richard's desk.

"So, no luck yet?" he whispered.

"Hey, I think I hear a hollow sound." She continued to move books, then knock. After a few minutes, she realized she looked and felt like an idiot. She spun to face him. "Could Rose be a kleptomaniac?"

"Ah...no."

"She doesn't need the money, but she certainly needs attention." And to Victoria, the idea of an inside job wouldn't die. "I keep coming back to the safe. How did the thief get in? I tried getting inside it today. Richard changed the combination and has kept it locked since Friday night to protect the rest of Rose's jewelry. No one's gotten inside. Including me."

"And you're an expert safe cracker, huh?"

"I'm as intelligent as anyone here."

He nodded. "More. But as much as Rose enjoys drama and the spotlight, she's not delusional."

Victoria sagged against the edge of the desk. "I guess you're right." She resumed her search of the bookcases. "You work on that side," she said, pointing to her left.

"I've got a better idea." He embraced her from behind, kissing her neck, sending sparks of need through her veins.

She rested against him, her needs and her goals never more at odds. "You're distracting me."

"What do you have on underneath this dress?"

She laid her hands over his, which was currently roaming her body. "You tell me."

"Nothing I can feel."

"Because nothing's there."

Twirling her, he pressed her against the bookcase. He lifted her dress, exposing her legs, which he wrapped around his waist. His pants slid against her inner thighs. "All I need to do is draw down my zipper, and I could be inside you," he murmured against her ear.

He was amazing. How would she ever let him go? "Search first, play later."

"When I find this idiot thief, I'm going to wring his neck."

She pressed a lingering kiss to Jared's jaw. "I'll help."

Though clearly not thrilled with her proposed agenda, he set her on her feet again and smoothed down her dress.

After a few minutes of pressing and knocking on the bookcase in various places, Victoria felt the far panel on the right side move. "It's here," she said, relieved and excited. "Help me push."

With Jared's added strength, they were able to shove the panel open, revealing the secret room. "After you, milady," he said, extending his arm and bowing.

"These costumes are getting to everybody," Victoria muttered.

The room was very small; Jared had to turn sideways to get in, and his head nearly touched the ceiling. Jammed inside was a filing cabinet and a small table holding stacks of paper.

Seeing little choice, they began sorting through the collection.

They found tax records, insurance papers and a stack of suggestive love letters from a woman named Christie.

Girl, Victoria corrected, noting the hearts instead of dots over the *I*s.

Secrets, maybe, but not the one she was after.

"This looks interesting," Jared said, holding an open file in front of her.

It held drawings of different types of machines. Most of them looked like alien doodles, but some were recognizable.

"That's obviously a fence," Victoria said.

"And this is a numbered panel," Jared added.

"Like the one the safe has," she remarked slowly.

Excited with the possibility, she thumbed through the

stack, and suddenly, there were the schematics for Rose's safe. A note had been scribbled in a corner: "Possible electronic fingerprint compromise."

"What the devil does that mean?" Victoria asked Jared.

"No idea, but it sounds like a definite flaw in the design."

"Well, well, well." She folded the papers several times and started to tuck them into her gown.

"That'll never work," Jared said, taking them. "I'll put them in my jacket pocket." He regarded her with a serious expression. "What're you going to do?"

"With you or the drawings?"

"Both."

"With them, I have no idea."

Would she really use them to blackmail Richard into giving her the contract if she couldn't find the necklace? She honestly wasn't sure what lengths she might go to. And for the moment, she didn't want to consider the possibilities.

"With you..." She looped her arms around his neck. "I've got definite plans."

BEING IN VICTORIA'S BED WITH her head on his chest and her fingertips tracing random patterns on his skin, Jared was sure he'd fallen into a permanent state of bliss.

The candles, once glowing brightly, now sputtered. His body was exhausted. The most complicated thought on his mind was wondering if he could summon the strength to pick up their borrowed clothes from the crumpled pile on the floor before the wrinkles needed professional help.

"Does that dress have a label sewn inside it?" he asked, brushing his fingers through her glossy hair. The vision of her standing before him in the candlelight was forever imprinted on his brain.

"I don't remember," she said sleepily. "Why?"

"I wanna contact the designer and see if he'll make four dozen, so you can wear one every day for the next month and a half."

She smiled. "I could just buy that one from Rose and wash it every day."

"But I wanna rip it off you every night."

"That's a better plan than…" She stopped and lifted her head. "How do you know the designer is a man?"

Jared's grin was all-telling. "How could he not be?"

She pressed her lips to his shoulder. "Your ideas are far better than mine. Richard should have put you in charge, since my grand scheme for recovering the necklace was a disaster." She turned to her side and propped her head on her hand. "Who took that stupid thing? And how the devil did they do it?"

Obviously her brain wasn't as easily led astray as his. He struggled to focus on the problem, knowing how important it was to her. He mirrored her pose. "The note about the electronic fingerprint probably has something to do with it."

"Sure, but who knows about that except Richard and his engineers?"

"Good point. The cops will figure it out, and you'll convince Richard to give you the contract even though he was an unfair, low-down creep for putting you in that position in the first place."

"I appreciate your confidence, but I don't think it's going to be so easy."

He drew a line over the curve of her naked hip. "I have intimate knowledge of your many talents." Richard didn't deserve even the professional ones. Though at least he'd been honest about his selfishness from the beginning. For obvious reasons, Jared didn't want to dwell on the comparison to his own actions. "I meant to ask you earlier…how'd you get the cops to do background checks without them wanting to come here and investigate?"

"Simple. We didn't tell him why we wanted the information."

Him? An alarm went off in Jared's head. "Must be a pretty close friend."

"We sort of have a history together. And don't even bother to ask his name. I'm not getting him any deeper into this mess than I already have."

"You're protecting him?"

"You bet I am. He's not the kind of guy whose bad side you want to get on." She scooted closer. "Jealous?"

"Intensely. What kind of history?"

"The professional kind. Besides, he has a thing for Calla." Abruptly, Victoria frowned. "Though the guy needs to make his move already. I'd have lost patience months ago."

"You like a guy who moves fast, huh?"

"Not usually, though you certainly did."

You did, too, he thought. She'd moved straight into his heart. No warning. No mercy. No going back.

He refused to believe there was no chance of her ever returning his feelings. Talk about needing a grand scheme...

AN URGENT SHAKE BY UNKNOWN hands woke Jared suddenly the next morning.

"Get up," a woman whispered harshly.

While Victoria snuggled closer, Jared opened his eyes a crack and vowed to kill whoever he saw.

It was Shelby.

So maybe he'd have to tone that down to simply ignoring his lover's best friend.

Closing his eyes, he turned away from her and buried his face in Victoria's hair.

"Oh, look, there's a seventy-five percent off sale at Barney's!"

Jared merely winced at Shelby's loud words, but Victoria lurched up, grabbing the comforter to cover herself. "What? Where?" When she saw her friend, she expelled a sigh of disgust and collapsed on the bed. "Go away, Shel. We're not hungry."

"I don't see how you aren't. Based on the trail of clothes I followed in here, you burned plenty of calories last night."

Under the covers, Victoria wrapped herself around Jared, whose body—despite the suddenly crowded bedroom—responded in kind. "And we could burn even more today. Goodbye."

"Sorry, honey," Shelby said impatiently. "Fun time's over."

"I sincerely hope Trevor is coming to this party today," Victoria groused. "You're downright mean when you're separated from him."

"I expect him anytime," Shelby promised calmly. "However, I came up here because I thought you might be interested in the fact that Detective Antonio showed up at the house this morning."

The cop friend, Jared guessed, now fully awake.

Victoria sat up again. "Devin Antonio? Dark hair, slightly tarnished badge, cranky disposition?"

Shelby nodded. "That's the one."

"Hell." Taking the comforter with her, Victoria hopped out of bed. "Where is he now?" she asked, waddling toward her suitcase as fast as the bulky cover would allow.

"Sitting at the kitchen table, drinking coffee and staring at Calla."

Jared wrapped the sheet around himself and stood. "I should probably get dressed and come with you." And make sure this guy's thing was solely for Calla.

Victoria's attention jumped to him. Her gaze roved over him hungrily, and he felt every movement of her eyes as if she'd stroked him.

Shelby snapped her fingers in front of Victoria's face. "Focus, girl. We've got a crisis brewing here."

Sending Victoria his own scorching look of promise, Jared slipped into the other room for his clothes from the night before.

Dressing quickly, he heard Victoria ask, "Who else knows Antonio's here?"

"Nobody yet," Shelby said.

"What's he doing here?"

"You know him, suspicious as ever. He thinks we're up to something illegal again."

In the process of buttoning his shirt, Jared peeked in the bedroom. "Again?"

Victoria stood in front of Shelby as her friend tied her yellow bikini. "Project Robin Hood, remember?"

Jared's mouth went dry. "Right. I, uh, guess I should put on…" He glanced down at himself, dressed in his shirt and pants from his costume. "Other clothes," he finally finished.

"The barbecue is today," Victoria reminded him.

Shelby patted his cheek as she strolled past. "How cute are you?"

"Keep Richard out of the kitchen," Victoria called after her friend.

"It's his kitchen," Shelby retorted.

"Tell him there's a gas leak."

Looking exasperated, Shelby crossed her arms over her chest.

"Fine," Victoria said. "Tell him your biscuit recipe is top secret."

"Oh, yeah." Shelby opened the door and headed out. "That'll work."

"What's happening to me?" Victoria wondered, leaning against the door and looking thoroughly frustrated—as well as irresistible. "I'm suddenly out of ideas. I always have great ideas."

"I can help," Jared said, his hands itching to run over her beautiful body. "First off, you might want to put something on over that bikini or your confrontation with this cop will be pointless."

"Pointless?" she echoed.

"He won't be listening. He'll be staring."

"I was going to wear a sundress over the bathing suit." She went to her suitcase and came up with a red one, which she pulled over her head. "I don't know why we're rushing downstairs in any case. There's no way I can keep Richard and the detective separated all day. It's finished. I'll never get the contract now."

The sundress didn't dampen his desire, but the defeated expression on her face twisted his stomach into knots. "Why don't you focus on a great proposal for the safe?" *Even if it doesn't work.* "Leave the necklace to the police."

"Sure," she said sarcastically. "Which one of my brilliant ideas should I choose to overcome the fact that the product doesn't actually work?"

"The one that doesn't mention the product doesn't actually work."

Victoria pointed at him. "That's smart. But I still can't deny I've been fooling around with you when I should have been looking for the thief."

The comment stabbed his heart. "Wasting your time?"

"No, I didn't mean that." She grabbed his hand. "My loyalties have been divided all weekend. It's incredibly frustrating, but I regret nothing."

"You don't wish you'd chosen Richard over me?"

"A week ago, I would have, but not now." Her eyes pleaded for understanding. "My career always comes first. So I *should* have been following Richard around every minute I wasn't involved in the search. Maybe I ought to wish I hadn't spent all my time with you, but I don't."

He stroked her silky cheek. How was he ever going to leave her? He was sure that once they separated and she went back to her life in the city, regret would follow. Regret she'd blame him for.

But he couldn't cancel his trip to Mexico. He'd given his word he'd be there. *Tonight.*

Part of him also knew he had to let her go if they were ever to have any chance of being together. She needed time and space, and maybe he did, too. His intense feelings were new and unfamiliar.

And even if she felt anything close to what he felt for her, he had to find a way to reconcile their opposing lives. He'd been considering new opportunities, cutting back on the executive adventure stuff. Maybe the next challenge in his life would be her.

"You couldn't have done any more than you did." He kissed her softly, then held her against him. Nothing he'd ever experienced had prepared him for the need of her presence, of dreaming so intensely about her love and devotion. "If it matters, I'm proud of you."

She clung to him. "It matters."

15

VICTORIA AND JARED HAD NEARLY reached the kitchen when Richard stalked into the hallway.

"Victoria, I need to speak with you privately."

This can't be good. "Can it wait?" she asked, trying not to sound desperate. "I'm starving, and Shelby promised me a biscuit."

She wasn't desperate. She was a dog.

"No, it can't." Richard leaned toward her and announced in a furious whisper, "The police are here."

She scrambled for a reasonable explanation and came up empty. Maybe if they hadn't stopped by Jared's room to let him change out of his costume, and she hadn't indulged herself by helping... Damn, she was deluding herself. The confrontation with Richard was inevitable. "The police? No kidding?"

"My office. Now."

Her head snapped back at his harsh tone, but she bit down on her anger and followed him along the hall. Jared stuck to her side as if glued there, and she could tell by his pounding stride that he was holding on to his temper by a thread.

Inside the office, Richard rounded his desk and sat, leaving Victoria and Jared standing on the other side. "You'd better have a good explanation for why a New York City cop is sitting at my kitchen table."

At Richard's condescending tone, her patience ended and her temper spiked.

"I specifically told you this matter with Mother's necklace was to be kept private." Richard's fierce gaze flicked to Jared. "But your judgment this weekend has been so questionable, I suppose I shouldn't be surprised you were unable to complete such a simple task."

That's it. I'm done being professional.

Jared started toward Richard, but Victoria snagged him by his wrist. "Thanks, but I've got this." When she felt his pulse pounding against her fingers, she took a second to indulge in a sweet shudder at the vengeful look on his face. It was aimed at Richard, the man who'd driven her to the edge of ethics and patience faster than anybody she'd ever known. She'd actually considered blackmailing him to get the contract.

She'd be so thrilled to leave this place, she could hardly contain herself.

Lifting herself on tiptoe, she pressed a grateful kiss on Jared's mouth. His fierce gaze swung to hers. "I've got this," she repeated quietly.

His lips lifted in a quirkly smile and he stepped back.

"Detective Antonio," she explained to Richard slowly, so he wouldn't miss any of the important words, "is a friend of mine, Shelby's and Calla's. The friend I wanted to call three days ago to report the crime that had taken place here. The crime you threatened me into concealing. The crime made possible by *your* safe failing."

"How dare you," Richard exclaimed in a furious voice.

"How dare I?" Victoria planted her hand in the center of his desk. "I literally broke the law to try to get your business. I asked my friends and my lover to go along with me. Everybody in this house has compromised their ethics to save your butt."

Richard's eyes spit fire. "Get rid of him."

For a second, Victoria thought he meant Jared. "Excuse me?"

"Tell that cop he made a mistake coming out here. There's nothing wrong. The necklace isn't missing. *My safe didn't fail.*"

At this point, Victoria couldn't believe she was astonished by anything Richard did or said, but she was. "You want me to stand in front of my friend, an NYPD detective, and lie?"

"I want you to take care of the problem."

"Oh, I intend to. I quit."

Richard looked confused. "Quit what?"

"I'm done with you." She dusted her palms together, in case the big words weren't enough to demonstrate her point. "I'm not taking any more orders from you. I don't want your contract. Case closed."

"You've lost your mind."

Victoria stood next to Jared and met his gaze. The pride in his eyes was worth twenty Richard Rutherfords. "No, I'm thinking clearly for the first time in a while."

Richard leaned back in his chair. His smile was smug. "I expect you'll change your mind after I have a very pointed conversation about your behavior with Leonard Coleman."

"Junior or Senior?" Victoria asked.

"Both."

"Good. Tell them I quit. I'm starting my own agency." She considered the fun she was having. A joy rivaled only by the hours she'd spent with Jared. "On second thought, don't. I'll tell them myself."

Jared bracketed her face with his hands and planted a hard, delighted kiss on her lips. "Wanna go find a thief?"

She nodded and let him lead her to the door.

Jared turned before they walked out. "You might want to shore up your alibi, Rich. This is about to get sticky."

"Wouldn't it be great if it was him?" Victoria commented, already looking forward to the very direct approach to questioning that Detective Antonio would no doubt employ.

"Nah." Jared pulled the door closed on Richard's sputtering protests. "It'd be more fun if somebody cracked his precious safe."

"You're so right. I never realized you had a bloodthirsty side."

"Anytime you want to learn everything about me, I'm available."

"In between death-defying adventures, anyway."

"Let's get through this adventure and see what happens."

She grinned. "I should hire you as my first employee. You continue to have all the best proposals."

Hand in hand, they headed to the kitchen, where, true to Shelby's word, NYPD's crankiest but most loyal detective was sitting at the kitchen table, looking at Calla as if he both worshipped and feared her.

At least something was normal.

"I'm sorry, he—"

Victoria held up her hand to stop Shelby's explanation. "You didn't do anything wrong. I never should have asked you to lie." Her gaze swept the assembled group and she felt a lump in her throat at the idea that she'd nearly compromised everything important in her life for some stupid corner office she could brag to her mother about.

She walked straight to Devin. "How's it goin', Detective? How's your Labor Day so far?"

"Fine," he said, clearly suspicious of her cheery tone. "Food looks good."

"It will be. Sorry to have to ask you to work, but there's an antique, multimillion-dollar diamond-and-sapphire necklace cursed by jealousy that's been stolen from Rose Rutherford's supposedly impenetrable high-tech safe. How'd you like to handle the interrogation of the suspects?"

Looking resigned, Antonio set aside his coffee cup and rose. "Hell. I knew the gang was on the loose again."

WHILE THE DETECTIVE WAS assembling the guests in the parlor, Victoria ran upstairs for her cell phone. She wanted to send an email to the Colemans—Junior and Senior—so she could book an appointment to resign first thing Tuesday morning.

She had so many ideas for her new agency she wasn't sure her brain could contain them all.

Hope for a possible future with Jared also dangled before her. A weekend fling that became a real relationship? Certainly not something she'd planned on, and not something that would happen without overcoming a great many challenges. But for the first time in years, she was excited about a connection that paid dividends to her heart instead of her bank account or résumé.

Now if only they could catch a thief...

Unfortunately, she couldn't find her phone anywhere in her room. She'd searched all the obvious places, such as her purse and luggage, when she recalled sitting on the chaise longue yesterday as she checked her messages. Sticking her hand behind the cushion, she felt around.

Her fingers scraped something hard and possibly metal, but it wasn't the phone.

With a strange mix of dread and pleasure, she pulled her hand from beneath the cushion and found the missing necklace clutched in her fist.

The gems sparkled with all their beauty and mystery as her mind raced through the possibilities of how the jewelry had found its way into her room. The thief had either panicked or grown a conscience. All she knew for sure was that a worried woman was minus a necklace, and a suspicious detective was determined to find it and its sticky-fingered thief.

At her urging, no less.

Understanding Antonio's earlier resignation at taking on an unwanted task, she headed downstairs. After hiding the necklace behind her back, she peeked into the parlor.

The guests, or rather, suspects, were perched in various poses of anticipation. Rose sat on the sofa with Sal on one side and Jared on the other. At least she'd get her necklace back.

The black-clad figure of the cop who'd come to judge them

stood alone at the back of the room, his handsome, Italian-featured face contrasting with his vivid Irish green eyes.

Victoria waved to him. Naturally, he looked irritated, but walked toward her anyway.

Jared also glanced her way, and she gave him a weak smile as she retreated into the hallway with the detective.

"What?" Devin asked. "I'd really like to have some of that barbecue. It's been a lousy few—"

He stopped as Victoria silently held up the necklace.

"That's the—" he began, only to halt at her nod. "You chicks are gonna kill me. Where'd you find it?"

Victoria was surprised by the wave of nervousness that shot through her. "In the cushions of the chaise longue in my bedroom."

"Has it been there all this time?"

She started to say no, but how could she be sure? "This is the first time I've seen the necklace since the night when Rose wore it to dinner. But when I conducted a search of everybody's room yesterday morning, I didn't look in my own room."

"Uh-huh. Calla told me you've been playing Nancy Drew all weekend."

"It's Robin Hood, actually."

"Robin Hood was a vigilante thief."

Victoria rolled her eyes. Spoken like a true cop. Still, she had to admit, "I suck at being a detective."

"But it looks so easy on TV," Antonio said sardonically.

"Are you gonna mock me or find the thief?"

"It would make my week if I could do both."

Victoria crossed her arms over her chest. "If you want barbecue before next month, you might want to move this along."

"Sure thing. You're certain you haven't added theft to your list of crimes?"

"My record's clean."

"Sure it is. Are you and that big guy with the tan sleeping together?"

"Y—" She stopped. "What does that have to do with the theft?"

"Nothing. Just curious. But anybody who spends that much time in the sun isn't working too hard."

"Really?" She gave him a knowing smile. "Is there a particular reason you haven't asked Calla out yet, or are you just scared?"

His green eyes sparked, then he visibly restrained himself. "Nice one, Vic."

She scowled. "I don't like being called Vic."

Shrugging, he stuffed the necklace into his jacket pocket, and Victoria had only a second to wonder who wore black leather at the beach in September before he'd returned to the parlor.

He stalked into the already tense atmosphere. "I'm Detective Devin Antonio, NYPD." When he held up his badge, several people exchanged uncomfortable glances. Emily gasped. "It's my understanding that a necklace belonging to Mrs. Rose Rutherford was stolen this past Friday night, and I'm here to find both the missing property and the perpetrator of said crime."

Victoria had to hand it to him. The man wasn't big on conversation, but he knew how and when to say the important stuff.

Richard surged to his feet. "This is Southampton. You have no jurisdiction here."

"Sit down, Mr. Rutherford." Antonio glared at him until he did, then again addressed the group. "This crime was reported to me by Victoria Holmes, who's a citizen of the city of New York and was concerned for her safety. Therefore, I'm making it my mission to find this thief and put a stop to the crime spree infesting this estate."

"Infesting?" Richard again started to rise, only to have Ruthie lay her hand on his shoulder.

"Let the police do their job," she said.

Richard sent Victoria a resentful glare, but followed his wife's order.

Maybe Ruthie was tired of her husband's posturing, and had decided to teach him a lesson. Victoria hadn't really considered her a suspect, but how could any woman be married to that narcissistic creep and not want to take him down a peg or two?

Before she could pursue her thoughts thoroughly, the detective began his questioning. With a precision Victoria admired, he ran everybody through their movements of the night in question. He drilled Richard about the safe and its capabilities. He asked Mrs. Keegan and all three Rutherfords about the property's security system.

"So, which one of you has it?" Antonio asked casually at the conclusion of the interrogation. When nobody moved, and in fact, all froze, he sighed deeply. "Come on, people. One of you did it. Fess up. It's a holiday, and I've got a date with grilled meats."

The only person who moved was Richard, who this time darted toward the detective before he could be reprimanded. "This has been a huge waste of time."

"Sit down, Mr. Rutherford," Antonio said, laying his hand casually on the butt of the pistol holstered at his side.

"Victoria already questioned everybody about their alibis," Richard pointed out. "Obviously, that got us nowhere, since the necklace hasn't been stolen, simply misplaced."

"I locked the necklace in the safe," Rose said wearily, as if tired of explaining the same thing over and over.

"I just don't see why we have to go through this farce of an interrogation when a crime hasn't even been committed." Richard gave the detective a haughty glare. "Though even if there was a theft, you don't have the authority to arrest anyone."

Antonio stared at him. "I'm sure I could dig out the paperwork for an accessory-after-the-fact charge that the local sheriff's department would be happy to file for me."

"If Victoria didn't find that necklace," Richard said confidently, "I can't imagine you will."

Dismissing Richard, Antonio walked to the center of the room. "Yes, well, as talented as Ms. Holmes is in PR, I have a few more skills than her in this particular area. Besides, it's not a matter of finding the necklace."

"Not find it?" Rose cried, clutching Sal's hand between both of hers. "But it's very important to me."

Antonio's gaze swept the room. "It's not necessary to find it, because I already have it."

Then, as casually as if he was pulling his keys from his pocket, Antonio held up the precious gems by their thick gold chain.

Though it was cool to see everyone's astonishment—especially Richard's—Victoria couldn't help being annoyed that she'd spent days looking for the thing, as well as being the one to actually find it, and Devin was getting all the credit.

"M-my necklace," Rose said slowly into the silence.

Victoria met Jared's confused gaze and suddenly wished she'd taken time to warn him. Surely he didn't think she'd been withholding the jewelry the entire time. Or that Antonio had found the thing in the twenty minutes he'd been on-site.

To her relief, Jared smiled and crossed the room to her. "Congratulations," he said, pulling her into his arms.

"Anybody else have a comment?" the detective asked, looking annoyed by the interruption of his big moment.

"Rose and I are getting married," Sal said proudly.

Richard whirled to his mother. "When did this happen?"

"Last night," she said, her face glowing. "With all this tension over my missing necklace, we agreed not to say anything until it was found."

"People, there's the small matter of who took the necklace in the first place." Antonio checked his watch. "I'm on a schedule here."

"But…" Shocked and pale, Richard sank weakly into a chair. "It's really been a most unpleasant weekend."

"Oh, get over yourself, darling." Ruthie crossed to her mother-in-law and kissed her cheek, then Sal's. "I think it's marvelous. We'll start on wedding plans immediately. Should we have the ceremony here on the beach? Shelby, can you cater?"

Shelby blinked. "Uh, sure. We'll all get together to discuss a date later in the week."

Rose, in her element as the center of attention, beamed. "That would be lovely. Thank you all so much for—"

David pushed to his feet. "I took the necklace," he said calmly.

Boy, it's always the quiet ones.

Sal was the first to recover from the shock. "But why?" he asked, his voice tight with pain. "Why would you steal from Rose?"

David sighed, and despite all the trouble he'd caused, Victoria actually felt badly for him. "I'm sorry, Mrs. Rutherford," he said, his pale skin flushing red. "It was an impulse. My mother was a secretary for Rutherford Securities, you see."

Victoria didn't—at all. By the blank looks on the faces around her, no one else did, either.

"When I was a kid, she worked there for many years," David continued. "She was fired when she caught her boss stealing supplies. She told the office manager, her boss denied the theft, the manager sided with her boss." David's shrug was slow and heavy. "We had to go on food stamps for nearly two years until she found another job. I saw Rose wearing that necklace the other night and all the old resentment came flooding back. I know it sounds bizarre, but I had the crazy idea that I'd take from the rich and give to the poor."

Finally, Victoria did see.

Detective Antonio, who recognized a valuable opportunity when it was presented to him, advanced toward David. "So you stashed the necklace in Victoria's room, hoping to throw suspicion on her?"

"No," David replied. "I just wanted to get rid of it at that point. I figured somebody would find it eventually, when I wasn't around. I'm sorry if you suspected Victoria."

"And the jewelry case in the pantry?" Victoria asked.

"What case?" Richard asked, confused. "When—"

"Be quiet and let him explain," she said, aggravated by his continual interruptions. Thank goodness she didn't have to work with the insufferable man.

David cleared his throat. "I sewed the necklace into the lining of my suitcase, where nobody would find it, so I had to dump the original box." He turned to Antonio. "I guess you're going to arrest me."

Victoria could have sworn sympathy skated across the detective's face. "Let's go see the sheriff, and we'll talk about what happens next."

But when Antonio started to lead David out, both Rose and her son stood.

"You'll do no such thing," the matriarch announced.

"Mother!" Richard exclaimed. "He broke into your safe. *My* safe, actually." He jabbed his finger in David's direction. "How'd you do it?"

David's shamed expression turned prideful. "I used my garage door opener to scramble the electronic signal. My mother told me the engineers at your company used to do it all the time to get into the executive lounge when they were working late. I could hardly believe it worked."

Victoria exchanged a knowing look with Jared. *Electronic fingerprint compromised.* By a garage door opener. No freaking kidding.

"That blasted, supposedly impenetrable safe." In a serious huff, Rose scowled at her son as she crossed the room. "You're not going to the sheriff's office," she said to David, grasping both of his hands. "Your poor mother. I can't imagine how she felt after her horrible boss lied, then doubted her word. It's difficult enough to be a single mom."

She kissed David on his cheek, then turned to Antonio with an inviting smile that had no doubt charmed kings and presidents for forty years. "Detective, surely we can forget all about this silly theft business."

By the expression on Antonio's face, Victoria could tell he was mentally repeating the words *silly theft business* as if Rose had spoken in a foreign language. But true to his sometimes odd and compassionate history, he sighed. "Fine. Whatever. I was never here."

He was in the process of leaving the room when Trevor, Shelby's fiancé, strode in.

"Sorry I'm late," he said. "Did I miss anything?"

AFTER TREVOR'S ENTRANCE, THE party pretty much broke up. Peter and Emily tried to console Richard, who remained furious with his mother, Devin, Victoria, Jared…well, pretty much everybody. Rose and Sal wanted to enjoy their holiday lunch during a private celebration cruise for two.

Jared, after recommending a certain secluded cove, had to leave for the airport.

Ruthie was kind enough to pack up containers of food for David, who went to see his mother, and for Victoria and her friends. They returned to the city and ate barbecue on the balcony of Shelby and Trevor's high-rise Chelsea apartment. Figuring they owed him—again—the gang invited the detective, too.

"I knew it was David before he said a word," Devin said, twisting off the cap of another beer bottle while the sun descended beyond the buildings at his back.

"How?" Victoria asked in disbelief, annoyed that Jared was on his way to Acapulco and that she hadn't ever considered David a serious suspect.

"When I started questioning everybody, he was the only one who was truly nervous. Also, when I held up the necklace, he stared not at me or the gems, but at you." He shrugged. "He was worried you'd be implicated in the theft, so I knew he was the one who'd hidden the necklace in your room."

Calla stared at him. "Why does that sound so easy?"

Devin lifted his beer. "'Cause it is. If you know what you're doing."

"Detective," Shelby admonished, reclining on the lounge chair with Trevor, "please keep the bragging to a minimum. We've had our fill this weekend."

"Sorry." The detective sent a furtive, longing look toward Calla that Victoria noticed, even if her friend didn't. "I don't usually."

Trevor kissed the top of his fiancée's head. "And yet everything came out well in the end."

Everybody turned toward Victoria.

"What?" she barked, grabbing her wineglass. "I'm perfectly happy. Why shouldn't I be? I didn't solve the case, plus I lost a valuable client, my senior vice presidency and my corner office. But I got my freedom. Life is damn near perfect."

"No, it isn't," Calla said, laying her hand gently over Victoria's. "But it could be."

"We have nothing in common," she told her friends, though ridiculous tears burned behind her eyes. "City versus country. Type A versus type B. He's off skydiving, for heaven's sake. And I still want my corner office. My own, mind you, but it's still necessary. I'm not facing my mother over Christmas dinner if I'm unemployed. You honestly think Jared and I could make it as a couple?"

"Yes," they all exclaimed at once.

For some reason, her gaze went to Devin's. His no-bull philosophy was what she needed to bring some clarity to the crazy, illogical feelings racing around her heart. "Detective?"

He shook his head. "I know about crimes, not romance."

Calla bumped shoulders with him. "Come on. You read people well. You've got an opinion."

"McKenna's a cool guy," Devin said, clearly uncomfortable. "He offered to take me deep-sea fishing."

Shelby sighed in disgust. "This ad for the Romance Network has been brought to you by the Repressed Detectives' Association of Manhattan. Perhaps we can get a word from their president. Oops, no, he's off strangling kittens at the moment. We'll have to get back to him later."

Devin pointed his beer bottle at Shelby, and even teasing, still managed to be threatening. "I'm *not* repressed."

Calla giggled. "The RDAM. They can be your first client, V."

"You chicks know how to cause trouble," Devin grumbled, though Victoria could tell he was going to give in to her demand for his opinion. "However, you also throw a good barbecue and serve a decent beer. And since McKenna's in love with you already, you're halfway there."

"In l—" Victoria sputtered to a stop. She wasn't sure she could even say the *L* word aloud. "How do you know that?"

Devin lifted his lips in what might have been an actual smile. "Pretty much the same way I knew David was the thief."

"Told you," Calla said smugly.

Victoria wasn't sure how to react. Her heart was jumping, and her practical side was fighting to convince the rest of her that she'd known the man only a few days, and it wasn't possible for seriously deep feelings to have dug in.

Yet she knew for certain that no man had ever challenged, understood and delighted her so much. Her desire for him seemed inexhaustible. His support of her efforts to find the necklace had been constant throughout all the ups and downs. He trusted and admired her as much as she did him.

Plus, he'd led her to realize how far she'd been tempted to compromise herself for Richard's business, when it wasn't remotely worth the sacrifice.

"Oh, good grief," Shelby said, slamming her hand on the arm of her chair when Victoria remained silent. "Get on a damn plane and go after him."

Trevor lifted his beer in a toast. "My corporate jet is fueled and ready for your flight instructions."

Victoria shoved back her chair. "Bye."

As she raced toward the stairs leading down to the apartment, she heard Calla comment casually, "You know, the necklace's curse might be real. David stole it because of his overwhelming jealousy for all the things he didn't have as a child."

Halting, Victoria turned to her devoted and always wise friends. "But I bet its future will be much more loving than its past."

As MOONLIGHT DANCED ON THE sand beneath his feet and a warm breeze skipped off the sea, Jared stared up at the ragged cliff he'd dived from.

He'd fallen, all right. And the ache in his stomach had nothing to do with entertainment for the restaurant diners who'd watched him jump while they enjoyed steak and lobster from the picture windows surrounding them.

He loved her. Why didn't she feel the same?

Their parting had been a brief kiss beside Detective Antonio's car, before he'd driven him to the airport. Jared's life called, as did Victoria's. But he'd been without her for a single night and already longed to see her.

He was so proud of her decision to start her own agency, but that would only mean more time in the city, managing her office and cultivating clients.

He had to be here. Or a facsimile of here.

The moon shone brightly, but his own light had dimmed almost to the point of being extinguished.

Being cooped up in a Manhattan office or apartment wasn't a state he could sustain.

But maybe if he was in Manhattan with her, the city would be brighter, even dazzling. And he was sure he could draw her away to see the parts of the world he needed to sustain him. Hadn't she relaxed beneath the sun? Loving his touch and their unique bond? Hadn't he been searching for a new challenge? Wouldn't she inspire him to realize a new dream?

As he rode up in the freight elevator that had been concealed beside the cliff for the divers, he embraced his new resolve.

He would convince her to give him a chance. Beg if necessary. Time and space be damned.

They would have a life together, no matter what he had to do to make it happen.

"A guest asked for you to stop by her table," the young maître d', Pedro, said as Jared stepped from the elevator.

Dripping wet, his mind on Victoria, and frustrated that he was stuck in Mexico for two more days before he could go home and claim her, he shook his head. "I'm due to go down again in twenty minutes."

Pedro grimaced. "Make an exception."

"Why?"

"Have mercy, *amigo,* she's stunning. She has on this dark green satin dress, and I swear she's naked beneath it. Frankly, how could she not be? I looked pretty hard, but—"

Jared raised his hand. "Fine." He held out his arms. "Should I go like this?"

Pedro's gaze raked him. Since Jared wore only a pair of soaking swim trunks, he doubted the restaurant manager would be happy if he dribbled his way through the elegant restaurant.

"She also tipped me fifty bucks," the maître d' confessed.

"Fine," Jared said again, feeling like a kindred soul with the love-struck kid. "I'll change and tell your lady how amazing you are, but you owe me a whiskey later."

"Absolutely."

"A good whiskey," Jared clarified, as he was in the mood for a nice, long brood among men.

He stripped off his swimsuit in the locker room, toweled off, then dressed in a pair of black pants and a crisp white shirt. As he walked through the dining room, the singer playing the piano launched into the classic "Somebody to Watch Over Me."

Not a song conducive to brooding men. Where was Sinatra when a guy needed him?

As he neared the table Pedro had indicated, however, Jared abruptly changed his mind. Pedro's lady wasn't his at all.

Sipping champagne, Victoria sat alone at the table.

Seeing her stunning face was like a caress to the melancholy feelings coursing through him.

"Hi," he said stupidly, still wondering if she was a mirage.

Smiling, she stood, and he noticed she wore a jade-green copy of the dress from the costume party. "S-sorry it took so long to get here," she said, her voice actually trembling. "A thunderstorm grounded my plane last night."

She'd tried to come to him last night?

The knowledge had him surrendering the last of his barriers. He would follow her wherever she needed to be. They would find a way.

She plucked at her dress. "I had to get a seamstress to make this. Silly, I guess, but what else was I going to do, stuck in L.A. overnight? It seemed important at the time to make a grand entrance."

"I'll take you any way you come," he assured her, clutching her hand in his, and knowing the two halves of his soul had been reunited.

She'd taken his heart with so little effort, and yet the hours they'd spent apart seemed longer than a day. He had nothing without her.

"I know this is sudden, and we haven't known each other long, and I'm not one to do things this impulsively, but when I want something, well, I pretty much—"

He laid his finger over her lips. "You're babbling."

"Twice in one week? What are the odds?" She threw her arms around him. "Anyway, I came to tell you I'm in love with you."

His heart took flight, rivaling even the exhilaration of cliff diving. "Are you?"

"Yes." She angled her head. "How do you feel about me?"

Direct as always.

"Up until three minutes ago, I was soaking wet with sea-water, missing you and feeling pretty lousy." Breathing in the scent of her hair, he held her tight against him, where she belonged. "But even then, just like now, I was completely in love with you."

She pressed her lips to his, and despite the public setting, lingered there. Her tongue caressed his, and her body, certainly bare beneath the dress, molded to his as if made for him.

Parting for breath at last, she gazed up at him, focused on him and him alone.

Whatever challenges lay ahead, he knew from that look that they'd climb or fall together.

"Wanna go back to the city?" he asked.

She glanced out the window to their left, where moonlight shone over the magnificent cliffs and beautiful blue-green sea below. "Nah." She tucked her head between his neck and shoulder. "Let's stay here awhile."

* * * * *

COMING NEXT MONTH from Harlequin® Blaze™
AVAILABLE JULY 24, 2012

#699 FEELS LIKE HOME
Sons of Chance
Vicki Lewis Thompson
Rafe Locke has come to the Last Chance Ranch for his brother's wedding, but he's not happy about it. After all, Rafe is a city slicker, through and through—until sexy Meg Seymour *shows* him all the advantages of going country....

#700 BLAZING BEDTIME STORIES, VOLUME VIII
Kimberly Raye and Julie Leto
Join bestselling authors Kimberly Raye and Julie Leto as they take you to Neverland—that is, *Texas*—in these two sizzling stories, guaranteed to make you want to do anything but sleep.

#701 BAREFOOT BLUE JEAN NIGHT
Made in Montana
Debbi Rawlins
Travel blogger Jamie Daniels is determined to show sexy cowboy Cole McAllister that she's not like all the other girls—in and out of bed.

#702 THE MIGHTY QUINNS: DERMOT
The Mighty Quinns
Kate Hoffmann
With just a bus ticket and $100 in his pocket, Dermot Quinn sets out to experience life as his immigrant grandfather had—penniless and living in unfamiliar surroundings. So the last thing he expects is to strike it rich with country girl Rachel Howe.

#703 GUILTY PLEASURES
Tori Carrington
Former Army Ranger turned security expert Jonathon Reece always gets the job done. This time, his assignment is to bring in fugitive-from-justice Mara Findlay. Too bad the sexy bad girl outwits him at every turn...including in bed.

#704 LIGHT ME UP
Friends with Benefits
Isabel Sharpe
Imagine walking into a photography studio run by the sexiest man you've ever seen and finding pictures...all of you. Jack Shea has captured her essence, but is Melissa Weber ready to bare even more?

You can find more information on upcoming Harlequin® titles, free excerpts and more at www.Harlequin.com.

HBCNM0712

REQUEST YOUR FREE BOOKS!
2 FREE NOVELS PLUS 2 FREE GIFTS!

red-hot reads!

Montana. Home of big blue skies, wide open spaces...and really hot men! Join bestselling author Debbi Rawlins in celebrating all things Western in Harlequin® Blaze™ with her new miniseries, MADE IN MONTANA!

Read on for a sneak peek of
BAREFOOT BLUE JEAN NIGHT

"OVER HERE," Cole said.

Jamie headed toward him, her lips rising in a cheeky grin. "What makes you think I'm looking for you?"

He drew her back into the shadows inside the barn. "Then tell me, Jamie, what are you looking for?"

A spark had ignited between them and she had the distinct feeling that tonight was the night for fireworks—despite the threat of thieves. The only unanswered question was when.

"Oh, I get it," she said finally. "You're trying to distract me from telling you I'm going to help you keep watch."

He lowered both hands. "No, you're not."

"I am. Rachel thinks it's an excellent idea."

He shot a frown toward the kitchen. "I don't care what my sister thinks. You have five minutes, then you're marching right back into that house."

She wasn't about to let him get away with pulling back. Not to mention she didn't care for his bossiness. "You're such a coward."

"Let's put it this way..." He arched a brow. "How much watching do you think we'd get done?"

She flattened a palm on his chest. His heart pounded as hard as hers. "I see your point. But no, I won't be a good little girl and do as you so charmingly ordered."

"It wasn't an order," he muttered. "It was a strongly

HBEXP0812

worded request. I have to stay alert out here."

"Correct. That's why we'll behave like adults and refrain from making out."

"Making out," he repeated with a snort. "Haven't heard that term in a while." Then he caught her wrist and pulled her hand away from his chest. "Not a good start."

"It's barely dark. No one's going to sneak in now. Once we seriously need to pay attention, I'll be as good as gold. But I figure we have at least an hour."

"For?"

"Oh, I don't know…" With the tip of her finger she traced his lower lip. "Nothing too risky. Just some kissing. Maybe I'll even let you get to first base."

Cole laughed. "Honey, I've never stopped at first base before and I'm not about to start now."

*Don't miss BAREFOOT BLUE JEAN NIGHT
by Debbi Rawlins.*

*Available August 2012 from Harlequin® Blaze™
wherever books are sold.*

HBEXP0812